VOYAGEUR

V*le*OYAGEUR
KIRK ADAMS

TATE PUBLISHING
AND ENTERPRISES, LLC

Le Voyageur
Copyright © 2016 by Kirk Adams. All rights reserved.

No part of this publication may be reproduced, stored in a retrieval system or transmitted in any way by any means, electronic, mechanical, photocopy, recording or otherwise without the prior permission of the author except as provided by USA copyright law.

This novel is a work of fiction. Names, descriptions, entities, and incidents included in the story are products of the author's imagination. Any resemblance to actual persons, events, and entities is entirely coincidental.

The opinions expressed by the author are not necessarily those of Tate Publishing, LLC.

Published by Tate Publishing & Enterprises, LLC
127 E. Trade Center Terrace | Mustang, Oklahoma 73064 USA
1.888.361.9473 | www.tatepublishing.com

Tate Publishing is committed to excellence in the publishing industry. The company reflects the philosophy established by the founders, based on Psalm 68:11,
"The Lord gave the word and great was the company of those who published it."

Book design copyright © 2016 by Tate Publishing, LLC. All rights reserved.
Cover design by Joana Quilantang
Interior design by Shieldon Alcasid

Published in the United States of America

ISBN: 978-1-68301-251-1
1. Fiction / Native American & Aboriginal
2. Fiction / Historical
16.03.04

1

THE TREES—OAK, PINE, and maple—all stood innocently as though they knew nothing about the body lying on the forest floor. The world was quiet, and there was no breeze in this part of the woods. It seemed as if the whole world had stopped when this man's life stopped, as if he were so important that all living things had to stop and meditate his existence.

The body was mutilated in the typical Indian fashion. It had been scalped, and anything valuable on the body had been taken. The head had been split by a tomahawk, and a Seneca arrow through the heart was the reason for the large patch of dark crimson on the man's shirtfront. This man's life had ended in a terrible way, but the saddest part of his story is that no one was out to find him: the garrison at Fort Niagara had more important things to worry about, and his body was behind enemy lines, anyway. No, his body would be left to rot in the woods of Western New York with the fallen leaves and logs. The promise and hope that he had brought to the New World would meet the end that met so many and leave the trees, the forest, and the world wondering what the life of this man had been like, what promise it had held, and what role he had played in the ongoing war for the continent.

2

It was a beautiful summer day in Paris, France, and the young man walking down the street was about as handsome as they come. He was tall, relatively thin with broad shoulders, and he carried himself with an air that few people possessed. As he walked down the street, he took notice of all the merchants lining the road, selling their wares: pots, kettles, food, clothing, and the like. The packed buildings held more merchants, but these also held lawyers, homes, and apartments. This was the poor part of the city, and the filth in the streets proved it. The children in rags darting between the crowds, the men and women with torn garments and dirty hair all showed just how hard life could be in the slums of one of the world's largest cities.

The young man reached a side street and turned into it. He walked for about two hundred yards then turned into an apartment. It was a dirty place. Some of his family were there huddled in rags and torn blankets. His two sisters were there with his mother. They all looked at him with somber feelings, for just this morning he and his parents had talked about the survival of the family. The young man knew that he had to get a job or get out. He also knew that there weren't too many jobs to be had, and none that would pay enough for him to help support the family. The only alternative that was left was to leave home. But where? If Paris couldn't support him at home, then how could it support him if he was out on his own? He had decided to take a walk, to see if he could find an answer. After about two hours, he had found one. Now he had to break the news to his family. It would be a long journey, and they were almost guaranteed to never see each other again.

"Did you find anything, Francois?" his mother asked.

"*Ou…Oui*," he solemnly stammered.

"What did you find?"

"I am going to travel to the New World."

"What? The New World? Francois! That is dangerous! I do not think that you should do that!"

"Mother, what else should I do?"

"We will talk with your father. Maybe we can allow you to stay here. Are you sure that you cannot get work here in Paris?"

"I am sure, mother, and you know that I cannot stay here because father cannot support all of us. You must feed Belle and Cecile."

"But what about the English? They are in the New World as well! They will try to kill you!"

"Mother, this world is full of dangers and enemies. I will make many friends there too. If I am afraid to go because of the English, then I do not believe I am brave enough to justify living anywhere."

Tears were brimming in his mother's eyes. Francois hated to see her so sad. But they both knew that New France was his only choice. Still, it would be hard to part. He was twenty-two. He had done various jobs in Paris ever since he was sixteen, but the last one had been almost a year ago, and that one was definitely not coming back. New France, a new life. That was the only option.

That evening, Francois broke the news to his father.

"What? New France? Son, was that really all you could find?"

"Yes, father. I looked around, and no one is hiring. I feel that New France is my only option."

"How will you get there? I cannot afford to pay your passage."

"I could join the army, but I might try to go on my own. I will figure that out tomorrow."

"Son, we love you, and we want the best for you. I agree that this is the best option, but you must understand why your mother and I hesitate in allowing you to go. The New World is full of dangers, and it will not be an easy life. You will make friends and enemies. You will have bad times and good times. You will face both sickness and health. Work hard, my son. Never give anyone a reason to call you lazy. No matter what happens, always remember that we love you."

Choking back tears, all Francois could say was, "*Merci*, father."

Early the next day, the docks were bustling as sailors loaded and unloaded cargo from the ships in port. The sun had been up for about one and a half hours when Francois came to talk with the ship captains. He needed a job.

"Say there, lad, get out of my way!"

"Watch it, son, you might get pushed into the water!"

Francois was surprised by the harsh language and the rough men who worked here and listened as they told stories to pass the time between jobs.

"Lad? Are you looking for someone?"

It was a captain.

"*Oui, monsieur*. I am looking for a ship heading to the New World. I would like to go there, but I need to find a ship to take me."

"Well, lad, I can't help you out. I do not head that way much, but I do know of a Captain La Coeur who heads to the New World frequently. If you are interested, I can arrange for you to meet him."

"*Merci, monsieur*. I would appreciate it."

"I have an errand to run right now, son. If you wait about half an hour, then I can take you to him. If you wish to see him now, you will have to go yourself. He is probably near his ship right now. It is that one over there." He pointed, and Francois liked the look of the one at the end of his finger. It looked like a good sailor, and Francois felt his heartbeat quicken a little.

"*Merci, monsieur*, I think I will go now."

"Good luck, lad."

As Francois walked toward the end of the dock where the ship was anchored, he felt excitement growing in his step. He walked eagerly and thought of the adventures that could lie in wait for him. If only he could find the—

"Can I help you, lad?" The sailor looked rough, but his way of speaking was polite.

"*Oui, monsieur*. I am looking for the captain of that ship." He pointed.

"Aye, lad, that ship belongs to Captain La Coeur. I am his first mate. Follow me, lad."

As they walked toward a well-dressed man, obviously a captain, Francois felt a nervous feeling in the pit of his stomach.

"Captain, this lad wishes to speak with you."

"*Oui*, son?"

"Captain, I hear that you often go to New France. I would like to go there myself and am wondering if you could take me. I would be willing to work, *monsieur*."

"Have you ever sailed on a ship, son?"

"Nay, *monsieur*. But I am a fast learner, *monsieur*."

"And what would you desire as your wage?"

"Passage, *monsieur*. The trip to the New World would be my pay."

"You have a deal, son. We leave in two days."

Two days later, the sun was shining brightly. The air had a cheerful feel to it, which contrasted greatly with the mood inside the apartment of Francois's family. They were all saying good-bye, and there were many tears shed by all of the family members, even Francois's father. It was the first time Francois had ever seen his father cry, and it was also the last. Francois was leaving indefinitely.

As Francois turned to leave, his mother gave him one last hug. His father shook his hand, and Francois felt a sense of manliness come over him, as if from his father's veins. As he stepped outside, he heard his father whisper one last phrase, "God be with you, son."

They all stood watching him leave. They watched until he rounded the street corner, and then there was no point to watching anymore. After some more tears, they all went back to their daily tasks. The oldest child, the first to leave, was gone.

3

THE SEA WAS choppy. It stretched as far as the eye could see, over many miles. It was a powerful force of nature that no man should dare to disagree with. Only those who worked with it, instead of against it, ever survived its fury.

As the ship bobbed up and down, Francois felt the movement in his stomach. He had not gotten seasick yet, but he was worried that he would before the trip was over. Try as he might, he could never be a sailor, even though he was learning the ways of the sea fast. He knew all of the orders, he knew how to work the sails, and he could climb up the rigging into the crow's nest. Still, with all he had learned, he knew that his life was one that desired to be on land. He eagerly awaited the landing in the New World, when he could help his country stake a claim in the rich and fertile soil and the fur-brimming dense woods. Many years from now, when the land was settled, he, his children, and his grandchildren could proudly say that he had been there when the land was wild and that he had helped to tame, shape, and build it into something that women and children could live in without fear. He was ready for the challenge, ready for the task. Yet, even as he thought of these things, his mind traveled back to his family in Paris and the home he had left behind. Had he chosen the right thing? Was he really heading in the direction that was best for him? For anyone? He could not tell. But he knew that if no tough, adventurous men traveled to the New World now, then no women and children ever would in the future. For many, this was the right choice. For him? He did not know for sure. Only time would tell.

"Lad?"

The mate's sudden words startled him.

"*Oui, monsieur?*"

"The captain wants the decks swabbed. We are nearing the coast, and the captain wants the ship to be spotless when we land."

"*Oui, monsieur!*" Francois called cheerfully.

They were almost there! They had been at sea for about five weeks now, and he was ready for the trip to be over. He could not help but be happy as he swabbed the decks, for he was in such a mood as would not let him be downhearted. He would soon be at his new home, searching for a living to be made. He had ideas, but so far none had really struck him as the right one. He was not worried, though. The right métier would show itself at the right time.

"Land ho! Land ho!" called the sailor in the topmast. It was Antoine, a young man of about twenty-five who had befriended Francois on the second day of the voyage. He was a good man, one whose future looked bright.

As the men prepared for landfall, they all showed excitement in the way that they worked. Even those who had worked grudgingly for the whole trip now worked with enthusiasm as they prepared to land.

They sailed the ship straight north for a spell to get around Nova Scotia. "The English own Nova Scotia," Francois heard another sailor say, "we don't want to land there." They sailed past Fort Louisburg, curved around the north end, and entered the Gulf of Saint Lawrence. They then sailed directly west, past some islands in the middle of the gulf, toward the shore of the Canadian mainland.

"How much longer, Captain?"

"Just one more day, lad, if all goes well. We should be landing soon."

As Francois lay down in his mattress that night, he felt nervous about what could happen on the morrow. *Tomorrow,* he thought. Tomorrow his journey to the New World would end. Tomorrow all of his work on this ship for the past month and a half would pay off, for he would have arrived at his destination. *Tomorrow,* he thought. *Tomorrow!*

As the rowboat came ashore, Francois could not help but notice all of the well-dressed men and women walking the streets of Quebec. By their looks, no one would guess that they were in a vast wilderness surrounded by natives. Francois hung around long enough to help the captain unload the supplies, then helped him load the ship back up with furs. "Fine furs," the captain said, "they will bring a good price in France."

After everything was loaded, the captain gave his men the freedom to go get drunk. Such was what all sailors did when in port. The captain knew this as well as anyone, and he was not going to interfere.

Francois did not go get drunk. He did not have one drink. He did not have the money, and the last thing he wanted to do was start out his new life in debt. That would never do. It was all he had been able to do to get here debt-free. There was no need to change that.

After a few hours of walking through Quebec, Francois was called to see the captain. Francois knew that this was good-bye, and he tried to show his gratitude to the captain. It was hard, for words could not express how grateful Francois really was, and he told the captain so. The captain just smiled.

"Son, you were a very good worker. You earned your trip and your wage. I am prepared to pay you well."

"You already have, monsieur, and I thank you very much."

"What do you plan to do?"

"I do not know yet, monsieur, but I will find something soon, I am sure."

"Son, you earned more than a trip over the sea, especially because you did not ride over as a passenger, but as a cabin boy."

"What do you mean, monsieur?"

"Son, I am going to give you several livres. Use them wisely until you can make more money. Son, never let anyone call you a slacker. You have the heart and soul of a real sailor."

Francois could not think of anything to say besides *merci*, so that was all he said. His eyes swelled with tears when the first mate put the silver coins in his hands. He said one last *merci* and then left. Captain La Coeur was the reason he was here, and Francois would never be ashamed to say it. He had never worked for a better man.

"Say, lad, might you be looking for work?"

"*Oui, monsieur*," Francois replied to this buckskin-clad stranger.

"Well, then," the stranger replied, "I have need for a young fellow like you."

"What kind of work do you need done?"

"I am a voyageur, and I paddle a canoe from Montreal to Fort Niagara at the other end of Lake Ontario. Sometimes I go farther west to Detroit and Michilimackinac."

"I would like to travel with you, if you need the help, but I cannot row a canoe."

"Paddle a canoe, not row, son. I can tell that you just came off a sailing ship! Anyway, I will teach you all that you need to know. Say, where are you bound?"

"I do not know, monsieur."

"Call me Alexandre."

"I do not know, Alexandre. I might look to work at a fort, but I would prefer to be free, not tied down to anyone or anything."

"Now that is my kind of boy," Alexandre chuckled. "I never was one for committing to long-term agreements. A man can never make his own decisions after that, it seems. I admire a young fellow who wants to live on his own. Independence is good, son. Say, what is your name?"

"Francois."

"I am glad to meet you, Francois, and welcome to New France."

"*Merci.*"

As the two of them walked to the shore, where Alexandre's canoe was, they both began to share stories of the Old World and the homes they had left behind. Alexandre had left no family, none at all. They had all died of a plague in the slums of Paris. After that, there was no doubt in Alexandre's mind that the New World was where he would live or die. It was his home now, and he knew no other. Francois looked forward to the day when he would do the same.

The next day, Alexandre and Francois left Quebec for Montreal, which was farther up the Saint Lawrence River. Though Alexandre paddled, Francois watched him the whole way, noting how easily he moved the paddle through the water, and how easily he made the boat go within half an inch of where he wanted it to. After a while, Alexandre began giving Francois advice about how to paddle the canoe—how to hold the paddle; how to direct the canoe; how to avoid rocks, logs, or other debris; how to know where there were sandbars or shallow parts, and on and on. Francois absorbed it all like a dry dishrag, but he still lost parts of what Alexandre told him. He could not help himself. It was too much for one day. Alexandre told him to never mind, for he would learn it all even better when he was paddling the canoe himself.

"I would let you try now, Francois, but I am in a hurry to get back to Montreal. I only left for a few days to check on an old friend in Quebec. I will not be going back there for some time now. Everything that I need I can get from Montreal or make myself."

After a few minutes more, Alexandre started singing. Francois marveled at his voice and how he made the words sound so beautiful. He could make them sound harsh or soft, whatever fit the mood of the song he was singing. He sang about voyageurs, lovers, France, and lost lovers. His strong tenor voice rang out with a clearness over the river, and Francois could not help but close his eyes to the world and focus only on what Alexandre was saying, singing.

He sings as well as he paddles, Francois thought to himself, *and I think he paddles better than anyone in the world!*

4

When Alexandre and Francois arrived at Montreal, the first thing they did was buy a buckskin outfit like Alexandre's for Francois. Though Francois had money, Alexandre insisted on buying it, urging Francois to save his coins for other things that he would need.

"What other things might I need?" Francois had asked him.

"How about you take a little walk around. You might find something."

Doubtful, Francois did as suggested. He had not gone very far before he realized what Alexandre was talking about. He only walked around for about thirty minutes, but by the time he returned, he had a tomahawk, long knife, deer-hide pouch, blanket, and no money. But he was proud of his purchases, and even more proud when Alexandre complimented him on his choice of items.

"You'll never be hungry or cold with a knife and tomahawk, son, remember that."

"I will."

"If you have the will to survive and the right tools, nature cannot kill you. But never get cocky. There's many a cocky man who has thought he could not die but did because he was not wary of nature's power. If used to your advantage, son, nature will never disown you. It is only when you try to work against it that you will have problems."

"So I made good purchases?"

"*Oui*, son. You will eventually want to get moccasins, but we can make those in the next few weeks when we have to hunt."

Francois couldn't help but be excited at the idea of making his own footwear. *In this country,* he thought, *a man has to learn to take care of himself. When he wants something he doesn't have, he either makes it or saves up to buy it.* How different from France! Though people still saved up to buy things, they didn't have the resources that the New World did. Francois had always wanted to live independently but had never thought it possible. Now here he was.

"Son, paddle a little harder to the left. You're drifting."

Francois was trying his hand with a canoe. Nearby, Alexandre was paddling a different canoe, watching to make sure that Francois learned right.

"As your paddle comes out of the water, twist it so that it comes out vertically. That makes your job easier, and it doesn't spray water everywhere. There you go, lad. That's the way!"

Francois had never guessed that there was a right or wrong way to paddle a canoe. How hard could it be? But, like with so many other things, he had been wrong. The two of them spent almost a whole day out on the river, paddling around. At the end of the day, Francois's arms and shoulders ached, but he was pleased with the progress he had made. Alexandre seemed to be pleased too, and he assured Francois that his muscles wouldn't ache after a few weeks of paddling and that the aches would be replaced by large muscles. Francois had never had large muscles, but he had seen many men whose muscles were ripping their sleeve's seams, especially on the ship from France, and he was excited at the prospect.

After two days in Montreal, Francois, Alexandre, and about two hundred other voyageurs launched their boats up the Saint Lawrence River, heading for Lake Ontario. Each *canot de maître* was loaded with molasses, flour, salt, cornmeal, and similar items for Fort Niagara, which was located at the junction of the Niagara River and Lake Ontario on the south side. Two smaller canoes carried special items in them for Fort Detroit. These were items that had been ordered by some of the fort's occupants, which included a new dress from France for one of the officers' wives, some mirrors and trinkets for another officer's wife, and then a package of a special brand of tobacco ordered by a group of soldiers. Alexandre and Francois manned one of these smaller canoes, and the other one was manned by two voyageurs named Eugene and Pierre.

To get to Fort Detroit, one had to pass Fort Niagara, canoe up the Niagara River, portage around Niagara Falls, and paddle along the north side of Lake Erie until they reached Detroit. Such a trip took a long time to make, and it took even longer than nature allowed because the voyageurs couldn't take the shortest route to Fort Niagara. The shortest route was along the south shore, but it was impossible to take the south shore because of an English fort that was located on it. "Fort Chouaguen," Alexandre explained, "is located on the shore of Lake Ontario that way." He pointed to the south.

"Couldn't we slip by in the night?" Francois asked curiously.

"Maybe, lad, but it isn't worth the risk. Fort Niagara needs these supplies, and our job is to get them there. We don't take any unnecessary risks."

Francois was disappointed. He thought it would be fun to run past a fort in the middle of the night. It sounded like an old fable, something classic that could be passed on for generations. And, best of all, Francois could always say that he had been there. Was he not going to have fun here? Where was the sense of adventure? After a few minutes, Francois asked as much of Alexandre.

"Francois, there is a big difference between fun and danger. Though you don't know it yet, you have probably never been in the kind of danger that you are in here. If you think that danger is fun, then believe me, you will enjoy your life in New France."

It wasn't the answer Francois was expecting. Nor hoping for. But deep down inside, he knew it was the correct one. He was disappointed, but he had a feeling deep down that he was going to be having some adventures here. Fun or dangerous, he couldn't tell; but he knew one thing: they were going to be one or the other, maybe both.

Day 2

Francois got up twenty minutes later than the other voyageurs, tired as could be. He admired their strength and discipline but couldn't imagine being in their position. He couldn't even paddle a canoe on his own yet, so how was he supposed to do it on limited sleep? Life in New France wasn't going to be a dance: it took *men* to tame this place. Francois knew this, but he was worried. He was worried about his capabilities, but he didn't need to be. He didn't know it, but down in his heart he was ready to be a man in New France.

"Pierre, load up your canoe. We're launching as soon as we eat breakfast."

"No hurry, Alexandre. If we leave a few minutes later, what difference will it make?"

"It could make a lot of difference, depending on the weather," Alexandre responded, anger creeping into his voice. He didn't like anyone challenging his authority, and those who did usually didn't stay on his crew long. He could find other men.

"I don't think it would make that much difference, weather or not," Pierre replied, respect and reverence carefully omitted. He didn't care if Alexandre got mad or not. He was bigger than Alexandre and was needed for this trip. After that, Alexandre may fire him, but who cared? "There will always be more opportunities," he said to himself. "I have enough skills to survive in this land and make a name for myself."

"We will leave in ten minutes, like it or not," Alexandre sternly stated. "And if you choose to use that time loading instead of eating, go ahead."

Murmuring to himself, Pierre hurried to finish loading. After a quick breakfast of jerky and corn cakes, they were on the lake. After a few hours, Francois took a turn paddling. He wasn't fast enough to keep up with the other boats, so Alexandre helped him. They paddled together, Alexandre directing, Francois propelling. It worked very well, and after a few minutes, they were at the head of the flotilla. Francois liked this work. He liked having the water splashing on his face, breathing in the fresh lake air. He liked the feel of the paddle in his hands, the feel of the canoe moving beneath him. He liked the rhythm of the paddling and the contented feeling he got from knowing that the boat he was on was moving, in part, due to his efforts. It was very satisfying work, and Francois had a feeling that he would be a boater for the rest of his life. Deep down inside, he thanked God for Alexandre and what he had brought to his life. He would never forget it.

As the voyageurs paddled, they sang to pass the time. They sang a wide variety of songs, ranging from love songs and breakup songs, to songs about life and hard times. Many were soft and sad, many were loud and fun. The voyageurs sang them all. Francois couldn't help but learn the words and melodies to some of the songs, especially the ones that were sung over and over. His voice wasn't very good, and he usually didn't like to sing, but it was all there was to pass the time. Francois especially liked the song "C'est l'aviron," a song about a man who takes his girl for a horse ride to her father's house, where she drinks to the health of those she loves.

> M'en revenant de la jolie Rochelle;
> J'ai rencontré trois jolies demoiselles.
>
> C'est l'aviron qui nous méne, qui nous méne
> C'est l'aviron qui nous méne en haut!
>
> J'ai rencontré trois jolies demoiselles
> J'ai point choisi, mai j'ai pris la plus belle.
>
> C'est l'aviron qui nous méne, qui nous méne
> C'est l'aviron qui nous méne en haut!

At the end of day 2, Francois was getting better at paddling, and he was also getting better at singing: he was becoming a first-rate voyageur.

Day 5

Francois was getting used to the schedule. He was still not enjoying getting up early, but there wasn't any way around it. If any of the men had a watch, it would tell them that they were getting up at about four o'clock, sometimes earlier. But since no one knew what time it was, no one knew any better. When the men were up and moving, they would start to load the canoes with the valuable items. When they set up camp at night, they would leave some items in the canoes, but the extra heavy or extra valuable items were taken out at night, as well as the personal items of the voyageurs. When morning came, reloading the canoes was the first job. The second was to eat, and the third was to launch the canoes for another day's worth of boating. It may sound boring, but it kept the men busy, and they were very good at what they did. Years of paddling had sanded away the rough spots, and these men were now professionals. This crew was one of the best of them all, as Alexandre, being a first-rate boater, only picked the best voyageurs for his crew. To be on Alexandre's crew was an honor, and all who had ever paddled for him knew it.

As the boats were launched, Francois asked Alexandre if he could paddle the whole day.

"Why sure, lad, paddle as long as you can. That's the way to learn! If you don't build endurance as well as skill, you won't be able to be a voyageur. *Non, monsieur!* Those two must go together, or you won't be able to handle the long trips."

Francois was glad to be paddling right away. His muscles were already larger, and they ached less than they had when the trip had begun. Alexandre directed the boat again, like he had for the past few days, and Francois took on the propulsion. He quickly got the boat out to the lead, and after a few more good strokes, he was there to stay. He was amazed at how easily the canoe was gliding through the water and was glad that he was part of the reason. Once he got into a good rhythm, he joined the other voyageurs in that day's edition of the singing. He noticed some improvement in that too, though he still had a long way to go before he could call himself good. As the morning wore on, the paddle seemed a little heavier, the strokes harder, but he kept going. He was getting tired, but he refused to quit. He knew that he wouldn't stay on Alexandre's crew if he couldn't paddle all day, so he fought on. It wasn't until it was almost noon that he looked back at Alexandre and was shocked to see that he wasn't paddling. The shock must have shown on his face because Alexandre laughed out loud at his surprise.

"Just noticed, did you, lad? I haven't been paddling for about an hour, and you have been doing a fine job. We are still in the lead, though the others have gained on us a bit. No matter, you won't improve if you don't try." And with another laugh, he started dipping his paddle again. Rejuvenated by the confidence that resulted from Alexandre's praise, Francois found himself dipping his paddle with more vigor than ever. After another minute or two, their canoe had gained more ground, and they were once again way out in front. That lead wouldn't be relinquished for the rest of the day, and Francois received much praise for his skill around the campfire that night.

Day 11

It began like all of the previous days had: early start, quick breakfast. Before the voyageurs launched their canoes, however, some Canadian Mohawk Indians came into the camp and demanded some breakfast. Though they weren't dressed for war, they still looked very fierce. Francois was frightened by them. Alexandre noticed his fear and motioned with his hand for him to stay calm. Francois didn't understand Indians, but Alexandre did. He knew that if anyone on the crew showed fear, then they might not be impressed by the French, and the last thing France needed was to lose their all-important Indian allies.

Though Alexandre was surprised at the boldness of the braves, he knew that he couldn't avoid feeding them. It would cut into the rations for Fort Niagara, and they couldn't afford to do that, so they fed them from their own personal supplies. As the warriors ate, their leader expressed disgruntlement to Alexandre; he was upset with the way the French were treating the Indians and claimed that the French were cutting the Indians short in trade. He claimed that the French didn't always give quality items for the beaver skins brought in and that some of the time, they didn't get enough items to make a fair trade either. Alexandre listened patiently as the Indian voiced his disgust then calmly apologized to him for the lack of satisfaction. He said it in Mohawk, which shocked Francois incredibly. It also shocked the chief. He stood there for a moment, mouth slightly open, a blank look on his face. He knew some French, enough to get by, but he didn't expect this common Frenchman to speak his language so fluently.

Alexandre knew he had the chief off-balance, so he continued his peacemaking speech by assuring the chief that there must have been some miscommunication and that the French did not mean to offend their Indian allies. He also assured them that the French would lower the prices and increase the quality of the products if the Indians voiced their disgust to the traders. To conclude his speech, Alexandre offered his hand, which the chief shook firmly. He was satisfied with the way the meeting had turned out and planned to take his anger to the traders. As the Indian party left, Alexandre mopped his brow with his sleeve and wiped his hand on his trousers.

"Time to launch, boys," he called, but there was not the usual enthusiasm and energy in his voice.

"What's wrong, Alexandre?" Francois asked curiously.

"That was a close call," Alexandre dryly replied, "much too close for my liking. The traders had better fix those issues that chief mentioned, or we will lose our allies. If we lose our allies, then we will be heavily outmanned by the English. What's worse, however, is that the Indians have adapted to our European products. They won't settle with going back to the way life was before. No, they will still want to get their cloth, kettles, fancy knives, guns, powder, and shot. If they aren't satisfied with our prices or quality, then they'll happily go to the English. That not only adds more strength to their numbers. It also puts enemies all around us. Our position in New France will be untenable because our forts will be stranded with no way to reach them. The war would definitely be over."

"So why don't the traders bring the prices down? And why doesn't King Louis send more soldiers?"

"One question at a time, lad." Alexandre chuckled. "The traders work for the king, and the king sets prices where he wants them. The traders don't have much, if any, say in the matter. Since King Louis doesn't know that the Indians are disgruntled, and possibly doesn't care, he won't lower the prices. And he doesn't send soldiers because he doesn't have them, or he is worried about sending too many over, for fear of England attacking France directly. Either way, it would take months for them to get over here, anyway, and if we ever get desperate for soldiers, we will need them a lot faster than he can send them. *Non, monsieur*, if we ever get desperate for soldiers, we will have to rely on Indians. They are the key to securing this huge continent. Securing them for the cause secures New France for the cause. They must not be lost."

Francois was impressed by Alexandre's ramble. He was a much better speaker than his buckskin outfit would suggest, and the way he emphasized certain words or phrases made you understand just what he meant when he said it. He could let you see into his mind by the way he spoke. It was a gift, and Francois enjoyed listening to him as their canoe rode the waves.

5

"How many more days until we reach Fort Niagara?"

"Just a couple more, lad. It usually takes about a fortnight and a few days, but I think we will be set back by a day because of that encounter with the Canadian Mohawks several days ago."

Francois was disappointed. He liked the paddling and the camping on the shores of Lake Ontario at night, but he was ready for the trip to be over. He was ready to live on shore for a few days, sleep in a bed, and eat some real food. He had lost count of the number of days since they had set out, but he knew it was somewhere around two weeks. In a few more days, they should have made it to their destination. Francois was looking forward to seeing Fort Niagara for the first time, seeing one of the greatest advantages the French had: control of the Niagara Peninsula.

The muscles on Francois's arms were now bulging beneath his shirt sleeves. They were hard and tough, built up from the daily paddling of the canoes and the daily loading and unloading of the cargo. They weren't the skimpy muscles of a French pauper anymore, they were the powerful muscles of a working Frenchman. Francois was proud of this fact and was proud that he had worked very hard for Alexandre. Alexandre had complemented him many times for his energy and drive, which pleased Francois even more, and drove him to work even harder. Whenever he felt like slacking off a bit or felt like cutting corners, he remembered his father's words: "Work hard, my son. Never give anyone a reason to call you lazy." Alexandre had noticed the drive that line had given him, as had Captain La Coeur. Neither knew what had given him the drive, but they both saw the result. And they both appreciated it.

Day 18

Francois and Alexandre were paddling at the head of the flotilla, their usual place in line. None of the voyageurs were singing today; none were joking or laughing. They were all ready for the trip to end and were glad that Fort Niagara was so close. They were anticipating the excitement of seeing old friends and eating real food. The baker at the fort was one of the best in New France, though almost anything would be better than the bachelor-cooked corn and flour cakes that the voyageurs had been eating for more than two weeks. Even though the voyageurs were not joking, they still were paddling with heart.

As Francois dipped his paddle yet another time, he heard the far-off sound of a cannon. He jumped in the canoe, almost falling overboard. Behind him, Alexandre chuckled.

"Nothing to fear, lad. That's just the Old Fort signaling to close the gates for the night. We will reach it tomorrow! Paddle to shore, men! Set up camp!"

Turning the canoe, Francois paddled for a small beach on the shore. He was excited but disappointed that they had not made it to Fort Niagara today. They were so close! Why couldn't they push just a little bit more to get there? Francois asked as much of Alexandre, who replied, "The fort is still miles away, lad. We wouldn't make it by nightfall, and even if we did, you heard the gun. The fort won't open until morning, whether we make it there or not."

Francois felt a little better but wasn't totally satisfied.

"How is the fort miles away? We heard the cannon, so it can't be that far away."

Alexandre laughed out loud so heartily that Francois started to laugh as well, though he didn't get the joke.

"Can't be that far away, lad? It most definitely is! Sound carries clear and far over cold water, so people miles behind us would have heard it too. Even then, have you ever heard a cannon, lad? Try standing next to one when it fires. You won't ever forget it. If you think that a musket is loud, don't ever stand by a cannon!"

If you think that a musket is loud…

Alexandre still hadn't forgotten the little adventure of a couple days ago. One of the canoes had been leaking from a scrape on some rocks, so the men had had to take a day off to fix it up. While they were so engaged, Alexandre had taken Francois out to hunt a deer so that they could make Francois some moccasins. After explaining how to load and fire the musket, they had found a buck grazing in a small clearing in the woods. Taking careful aim, Francois had downed the buck with a shot right through the heart. He had jumped like he was snakebitten, though, when he heard the bark of the musket. If the gun had sounded before the bullet left it, then Francois would have missed the buck by yards. The whole thing had seemed really humorous to Alexandre, who had been joking about it ever since it happened.

As Francois lay awake under his blanket that night, he gazed up at the stars and wondered if his family was all right back in France. He thought back to the smelly, dirty apartment, and how hard it had been to find food and keep clean. It was easy to get sick, and there was no way of getting medicine. Francois knew that his life was better off here in New France, but he could not help but miss his family and the possibilities he had left behind in

France. After all, he was still a Frenchman, and that would not change. He was here for France and God, and he was going to take his job seriously. After he had lain awake for about two hours, he fell asleep.

The sun was up. Francois felt its golden warmth on his face as he opened his eyes. Already many of the voyageurs were moving about on the shore, some loading canoes, some getting breakfast, some just loafing. After stretching out his legs and arms, Francois went to join them. He started loading a canoe but was stopped by a rough reprimand from Pierre.

"Leave that canoe alone, lad! That's my boat, and I will do my own loading! Now get away!"

Francois did as told but could not help but be hurt by Pierre's scolding. He was just trying to help, and Pierre was loading slower than everyone else. Hurt as he was, however, the excitement of reaching Fort Niagara before day's end quickly eliminated any sad feelings in his mind, and after loading his canoe up, he ate a hurried breakfast. Alexandre noticed his eagerness and told him that patience would serve him well.

"Son, there is no need to hurry. We will definitely be at the Fort by nightfall, so take your time. Eat your fill of breakfast because you will need the strength today."

Francois still didn't eat as much as usual. Why would he need a full day's strength? Alexandre had said that they wouldn't be paddling all day. Why bother? Besides, Francois was too excited to eat much, anyway. His stomach was fluttering, and he was ready to start paddling.

Several hours later, as the flotilla rounded a slight bend in the shore, Francois glimpsed the flag of France flying on a pole. The day was very cloudy with a thick shroud of fog, so visibility was poor, but Francois figured that below the flag was Fort Niagara. He asked Alexandre, who replied, "Good eyes, lad! There she is, boys, we are almost there!"

Francois paddled faster despite his growing lack of energy. He was beginning to feel the punishment for not eating his share of breakfast. *Oh, well*, he thought to himself, *at least I am almost there. The excitement will get me there, and then it will be over with.* Little was he prepared for what was to come.

All was quiet inside Fort Niagara. Inside the French castle, the commandant was enjoying a fine meal with his officers. They were dining with the usual pomp of the French officers in New France: golden goblets, china, multicourse meals, and all the little details that made their meal just like one the wealthy would enjoy in France herself. Though life on the frontier was rigorous, being an officer was rewarding, and many officers lived lives as fine or better than they had in France. Such were the privileges of rank, and such were the lives of officers.

As the commandant enjoyed his wine and company, three French soldiers patrolled atop the earth and stone ramparts, scanning the woods for enemies. Often, their gazes would also roam over the horizon of Lake Ontario, searching for boats or ships, friend or foe, that would bring supplies or trouble, depending on the nationality. As these three men paraded in their never-ceasing walk, two others stood at the gate of the Six Nations, allowing no human to enter without a password, papers, or a direct order from the commandant. The only exception to these three qualifiers were Indians, who were usually allowed in, but only in small groups. Besides these five guards, there were others keeping lookout, though not in as strict a fashion. There were men atop both the north and south redoubts, both of which offered a wide field of view to lookouts, and there were men patrolling the fort's lakefront as well, who kept a loose watch of any approaches to the fort by water. Besides all of these men, several off-duty soldiers and citizens were wandering about on the parade grounds, and many of these were also looking to the lake.

It was late in the fall, and the fort was anxiously waiting for its winter supplies. Everyone in the garrison knew that, from the commandant down to the Indian child living in the village at the landing, all of the fort's inhabitants needed the supplies of the expected flotilla. The fort's survival depended on the voyageurs, and the result was peeled eyes whenever eyes looked at the lake.

It was a young soldier named Bertrand who saw them first. He was walking from his bunk in the north redoubt to the bakehouse to chat with Alphonse, the baker, who was a good friend of his. As he walked, he glanced out over the lake, expecting nothing but hoping everything. Thus was his surprise even greater when, through the fog, he saw two canoes paddling toward the fort. His first reaction was one of surprise, then fear, for he suspected that the two canoes were spying. His fears were calmed quickly, though, as after a few moments, more canoes came into view. Reassured, Bertrand's face lit up with a smile as he ran to the bakehouse. He opened the door just in time to see Alphonse taking bread loaves off their cooling racks and putting them into bins. The light in Bertrand's eyes told most of the message by themselves, as Alphonse knew Bertrand so well that he could almost read his mind. Two quick sentences told the rest.

"A flotilla is coming in! Come to the landing to unload!"

Leaving the rest of the loaves, Alphonse followed his excited partner out the door. As they ran toward the gate, they glimpsed other people running from all places in the fort—some from seeing the flotilla, some just from hearing that it had arrived. They all ran down to the landing on the Niagara River next to the fort, where a small Indian village was situated. This was the closest place to the fort where boats could be unloaded, as the fort sat higher than the lake. As Francois pulled up his and Alexandre's canoe, he felt important to have all of these people running up, excited about the arrival of the flotilla. He couldn't believe how many people lived in the fort as about one hundred currently lined the shore, waiting for the boats to land.

As the boats hit the dirt of the landing, the unloading process began. Alexandre immediately took charge, directing the men as they handed their supplies to the fort's eager inhabitants. When someone had received a parcel, he began to trek up the hill to the fort where the supplies were kept. Soon these people formed a large parade, with fifty to a hundred men taking supplies to the bakehouse, castle, and storage rooms.

Francois found it hard to carry the loads that many of these men carried. Some of the men took packs that weighed almost one hundred pounds; some of them took two. Francois had to settle for lighter packs, though the ones that he carried still weighed sixty-five or seventy pounds each. As Francois walked, he admired the uniforms of the French garrison, noticed the practical yet decorative clothing of the Indian men and women, and laughed at the Indian children running around in the grass, playing with sticks and balls. Life at the fort appeared to be very active, and Francois was enjoying his first impression of it.

When these supplies had been put away, the talk began. The voyageurs began to tell stories of Montreal and Quebec, the soldiers of the fort told about the Indians, and all told of unusual happenings that had occurred since their last meeting. The fort was a bustling place with excited chatter in every building and joyful laughter ringing out from every corner. For the voyageurs, being in the company of women and gentlemen was something they had lived without for almost three weeks. For the fort's occupants, the supplies that the voyageurs had brought made their rough manners worth the tolerance.

Alexandre paid Francois well for his work. He also offered him another job when he returned from Fort Detroit.

"I have Eugène and Pierre coming with me, and they will be enough for this trip. But when I come back, I will be putting a new group together, and I would be more than happy to have you with me."

"I would like that," Francois replied enthusiastically. "But what will I do between now and then?"

"The rest of my crew will be heading back to Montreal in a few days. You may go with them if you like. I will look for you there when I return. Or, if you would prefer, you may stay here at Fort Niagara. I will look for you here when I return as well."

"*Merci*, Alexandre. You are the best person I could have hoped to meet here. You have given me the chance to make it in this wilderness, and I am very grateful."

"You are a good lad, Francois, and a good worker. Do not let anyone ever tell you that you are lazy because you do not have laziness in you. You worked harder than many men twice your age and size but did not complain. I just wish there were more men like you in this world. Such men are needed."

As Alexandre walked away, his words echoed in Francois's mind: "Do not let anyone ever tell you that you are lazy, because you do not have laziness in you." It was very similar to what Captain La Coeur had told him on his last day of work. Francois knew he was leaving an impression in the minds of both of these men, and he was proud of that fact. He was living up to his father's challenge: "Work hard, my son. Never give anyone a reason to call you lazy." And he was glad that his father's legacy was being carried on. Suddenly, while standing in the great parade grounds of Fort Niagara, Francois wondered what had become of his family. Were they still living in the smelly old apartment? Had they moved to another? Or had they, by some stroke of luck or blessing, upgraded into better living conditions? Francois knew that he might never know the answer, but he still could not help but wonder what had and would become of his family.

Two days later, Francois stood at the landing below the fort to wave Alexandre, Eugene, and Pierre away. As their two canoes disappeared up the Niagara River, Francois sighed deeply and thought about Alexandre—the only reason that he was alive today. If it had not been for Alexandre, then Francois would probably still be in Quebec looking for work. He had learned many skills of survival from Alexandre, but he still had many more to learn, and he decided that he was going to begin now.

6

ON THE NEXT morning, Francois was up with the sun. He had slept on the parade grounds under a deerskin blanket, and he could feel the difference that sleeping outside made. He was stronger and better rested, and the fresh air put him in a good mood as he breathed it in. Grabbing some jerky from his shoulder pouch, he ate it knowing it could be all he would eat for many days straight. His mind was fresh, and his mind was made up: he was going to scout the country. Using the money that Alexandre had paid him, he bought himself a musket and forty rounds of ammunition, and then with his tomahawk, knife, and blanket, he headed out.

After saying good-bye to Alphonse and Bertrand, who had become his good friends, he started traveling up the Niagara River toward the falls. Though following the river to maintain his course, he stayed inland a little ways so that he would not easily be seen by anyone on the opposite shore. After walking for a couple of hours, he sat down to eat. He ate some more jerky and then went down to the river for a drink. After drinking, he headed out again, this time heading more inland. He was exploring and wanted to get to know all of the country as best he could.

In the middle of the afternoon, Francois had to climb up onto the top of the gorge that the Niagara River is located in. As he started going up, he felt strong and confident in his ability to reach the top, but as he got closer and closer to the top, his strength slowly gave out. When he had gone about two-thirds of the way up, he felt that he could not go on any longer. However, taking a deep breath, he somehow found the strength to continue. Five minutes later, he was lying on the ground at the top, panting. He had made it but had lost much strength in the process. He decided that he had gone far enough for the day and made camp under a small group of oak trees. He built a small fire, more for cheer than heat, and ate some more jerky to silence his complaining stomach. Tomorrow he would have to hunt, for his jerky supply was running low, and he would not survive long in this wilderness if he could not hunt. He was a little unsure of his ability to hunt and skin a deer on his own, but he did not plan to starve. On the morrow, he decided, he would go hunting.

The woods echoed the shot. Francois walked up to the fallen deer and felt an exhilarating sense of self-reliance in the knowledge that he had killed a deer on his own. Drawing his knife, Francois got to work on the bloody part. After he had skinned the body and taken the choice cuts, he wrapped the meat in the hide and headed off into the woods, leaving the rest of the carcass behind. He knew that foxes or wolves would eat the rest, as no creature would turn down a free meal such as that. Of course, it might take a few hours, as the animals wouldn't approach when the smell of humans was so strong, but when the smell had faded, then the bones would be picked clean.

After reaching the Niagara River once again, Francois followed it a little ways to a small fort that was situated along the trail. He had never heard of this fort, but he knew that it was too close to Fort Niagara to be English. Approaching it, he noticed a few Indian women out scraping hides, some Indian children playing, and, at the other end of the clearing, two French soldiers were returning with two turkeys. Francois liked the fort immediately and hailed the soldiers as they reached the entrance.

"What fort is this?" he asked.

"It is Fort Little Niagara," one of the soldiers replied. "It guards the portage over yonder, the one that you must have climbed to get here."

"I climbed it, *monsieur*," Francois said, "but it was not easy. 'Twas something that I should not like to do again for a long time."

"And you shall not have to," the other soldier stated very matter-of-factly, "if you do not go back down. Now, then. Why do you come here? Do you have a message from Fort Niagara?"

"*Non, monsieur*. I came to Fort Niagara with Alexandre, a voyageur. But he went on to Fort Detroit a few days ago."

"*Oui*, he passed by here on the way."

"When he returns, I shall go back with him to Montreal, but until he returns I am going to traverse the country and get to know it. One of these days I may even own a piece of it."

"Perhaps, lad, perhaps," the older soldier mocked, "but I would not expect it if I were you. King Louis would not let a square foot of this land go if he knew its worth. This land has much beaver, fox, and mink, and all draw large markets in Paris. This land is worth more than even King Louis knows, and though someday ordinary people may have their own plots of it, this land will belong to none other than the king himself for many years."

Francois knew this, but somehow he knew that this land would hold many common people, support many different cultures, and give many people second chances at life. In Europe, there wasn't enough land for all to have their own. But here, in this new world, all people could own their own plots with land to spare. No white man had yet found the end of the continent, if there was one, and the land only got more open and spacious the farther west you went. At least, that is what the Indians and voyageurs said.

Francois found Fort Little Niagara very much to his liking. It housed about one hundred people, including the small tribe of Indians who lived outside of the fort's walls, but the fort's size did not accurately reflect the fort's strategic value. Any Frenchman wishing to travel to the western forts would have to pass this location, and the English would be aware of that fact. Therefore, Fort Little Niagara was one of the most strategically located forts on the continent. Francois, though not a military strategist, knew the importance of such ground and was impressed by the small fort's position.

When he got to the trade house, Francois found several Indians there trading for European items. Francois watched the trading with keen interest, as it was unlike anything that he had ever seen. He enjoyed seeing the different items that the different Indians traded for. Some traded for beads, some traded for iron kettles, some traded for blankets, some for cloth (red was the favorite color), and still others traded for weapons. Knives, tomahawks, and muskets were very popular items in the trade buildings of New France, and Francois saw many Indians leave the fort armed with European potential. He knew that it would not be long before the Indians would shoot as well or better than the European invaders, and he considered the problems that might arise from such a circumstance. If the Indians were better at European warfare than the Europeans themselves, then there was a chance that the Europeans would end up being driven off the continent. Francois did not believe it would happen, but one could never be too sure. The Indians were not to be taken lightly.

After the Indians had left, some happy with their trades, some upset by the cost of the higher-end items, Francois talked business with the trader. He did not have much, but his deerskin hide was very valuable, and he could tell that the trader wanted it.

"Son, I don't know if that deer hide is worth cornmeal, flour, *and* salt. I think that you are asking too much."

"Well, suit yourself. I would not wish to rob the king of France of the goods in his storehouses, no matter how far from France we are. *Non, monsieur,* winter's coming. I may well need this hide as another blanket in a month or two. *Je suis desole* to have bothered you, but I wanted to get an idea of what it would be worth. Now then, I think I must be going. I want to get a good start—"

"Now wait just a minute. If you are so set on keeping that hide unless you get cornmeal, flour, *and* salt, then I think I'd better give you all three. It is a fine skin, and I do think that it will fetch a fair price, so I'll not bargain anymore and give you the price you asked."

Francois nodded. He knew that the hide was better than the trader had admitted, and he knew that the trader thought so.

"I also need a small frying pan. I will pay coin for that." Francois felt a strong sense of victory as he walked out into the sunshine with sacks of cornmeal, salt, and flour, as well as his frying pan. Putting them into his shoulder bag, he headed outside the fort to make camp for the night.

After he had built himself a fire, Francois cooked some cakes with his cornmeal. He added some salt for flavor and then ate some of the remaining deer meat as well. It may not have been much of a meal, but Francois had worked for every bit of it, and to him it equaled a feast. As he lay awake that night looking at the stars, he made the decision to move out at first light, heading south.

The sun was just beginning to peek over the eastern horizon when Francois shouldered his pack and headed out on the trail. Glancing back, he saw Fort Little Niagara standing firm, not fully awake. There was smoke rising from the chimney, and one of the Indian maidens had gone to a nearby stream for water, but no one else appeared to be up yet. Turning back to the trail, Francois moved on.

The woods were alive with activity. Squirrels chattered from every oak tree, chasing each other up and down the trunks. Now and then, a deer appeared, but always out of musket range. Chipmunks ran along fallen logs, looking at Francois with their striped faces, and now and then Francois glimpsed a rabbit. As Francois walked, he noticed that the roar of the falls of the Niagara River was getting louder. Knowing that he must be close to them now, and curious to see their beauty, Francois turned west. He had not gone far before he came out of the woods to the river's edge. Just slightly to the north, there was mist rising, and Francois correctly guessed that this mist was right above the falls. Turning back into the woods, he headed north for about half a mile and then came to the river's edge yet again. This time, he was right next to the falls.

Francois watched the water spill over and was amazed at the beauty of this natural cataract. The white foam on top of the water made the river look lighter than it actually was, but Francois knew that this river was dark and beautiful. Kneeling down, he took a long cool drink from the raging water and enjoyed the feel of it falling down his esophagus, almost like it did over the falls. The feel of the mist and the cool droplets that splashed onto his face when the water hit the rocks sent shivers up Francois's spine, and he stood there for several minutes, just taking in the panorama around him.

As he watched the river, Francois caught a slight movement on the opposite shore. Looking up quickly, he saw two people at the river's edge on the other side. They were too far away for features to be made out, but they appeared to be Indians. Slowly backing into the woods to not draw attention, Francois disappeared into the brush. He would rather not be seen.

Observing from his new position, Francois watched the falls for another five minutes before turning back into the woods. They were an amazing piece of nature, and Francois knew that he would come back to see them many times in the future. This trip was working wonders for Francois's physique and self-confidence, and he was becoming more and more of a naturalist with each passing day. He was learning all he could about survival, and survival itself had taught him even more than that. However, he had not encountered any dangerous circumstances yet, which are the real test of a man's durability.

He was walking down a very old trail through a stand of maple trees when he came face-to-face with a group of five or six Indians. All had painted faces, and all looked fierce and wild. All had tomahawks and knives on their belts, but Francois noticed that some had fresh scalps hanging as well. They looked him up and down, as if deciding whether he was worth killing or not. Francois knew that fear would lead to death, so he tried to act brave. One of the Indians gave a grunt, and then another lifted his bow.

7

Francois's eyes grew wide, and he turned to run, but one of the fiercest-looking braves pushed the warrior's bow aside and then sternly spoke.

"Do not fear us, Frenchman," he said. "We are Seneca and will not harm any man who is our brother. The French are our brothers, so you are our brother also. Come join our fire tonight."

Francois nodded, but he was still nervous. He had just come very close to injury, possibly death, and his heart was still returning to its normal cadence. As the Indian group turned to leave, Francois found himself walking in the middle of a single-file line down the old narrow trail. The Indians had obviously used this trail before, as they walked it with confidence and speed that amazed Francois. He struggled to keep up with those ahead and not be kicked by those behind, who were following on his heels much closer than he liked. The leader of the group, the one who had pushed the bow and spoken to Francois, was walking in the lead right now, and Francois noticed that the other Indians were very wary of the woods around them. When Francois mentioned this out loud to himself, the Indian right behind him, the one who had raised his bow, said, "There is a party of Mohawk warriors in these woods, and we do not wish them to ambush us."

"I did not know that Mohawk Indians came this far," Francois replied honestly. "Do they seek scalps or prisoners?"

"Both," the warrior solemnly answered, "and I fear they will attack our village if we do not return soon. It is still two suns away."

"Are the Mohawks fierce?"

"Very fierce, but no fiercer than any other native in this land. Many of my brothers have fallen while attacking the English and Mohawk who live over where the sun rises. Some have gone as far as the great village of Albany."

Francois had heard of the town before while at Fort Niagara. It was one of the largest towns west of New York, a city that was located on the Atlantic Ocean. If the Seneca warriors had traveled all the way to Albany, wherever it was, then it was no real surprise that the Mohawk warriors were traveling this far. After all, if the Seneca were taking prisoners and scalps, then the Mohawk numbers would be dwindling. They would need prisoners to fill the ranks and scalps to even the combat strengths. Francois knew that neither side would stop raiding until this war ended and the tribes were at peace once again. If the war ended, however, then one army, one nation, one king would control most, if not all, of North America. Both New France and the American colonies would be one country, and the controlling European country would be the world's superpower. Francois knew all of this, and yet he still doubted that one country would one day control the whole continent. It was too big for that.

The Indians leading the column stopped suddenly. Francois looked around quickly, but he did not see anything out of the ordinary. Still, he decided to trust the Indian instincts more than his own. They had been here longer than he had, and they knew the ways of the woods and the Indians that they faced; and Francois knew better than to distrust them. It could mean life or death.

The Indians started on moving more slowly this time. Francois noticed that every warrior was alert, eyes peeled for movement; every Indian with a gun had it up, poised for action; and those who didn't had arrows on their bowstrings ready to be drawn back and released. Francois's gun was not loaded, and he found loading while on the move to be much too hard for him, so he drew his knife instead. It would make a good projectile if he needed to hit someone at a distance. After that, his tomahawk would be his close-quarter weapon, or he would use his musket stock as a club.

Glancing around nervously, Francois now noticed that the woods were quieter than they had been before. Was that what had alerted the Indians? Francois didn't know, but he definitely wondered. The little things can mean everything in the woods, and the Indians had become aware of danger somehow. Francois decided to ask them about it later, when they were together in camp. If he survived until then.

They were just rounding a very large pine tree when Francois noticed a deer move off to the left. After it had disappeared, Francois's memory of its movement and appearance made him question if it was really a deer. The other Indians had not seemed to notice, so Francois figured that it was a deer. Still, one must not be too careful.

There were some fallen logs lying about now, and some of them were thick and old. Some still had the bark on them, some had the bark peeling off, and some were completely bare, with grooves running through the inner tree layers where termites and other insects had burrowed long ago. It was behind one of these logs that Francois noticed motion. Looking at the log, he saw several red feathers disappear below it, and he knew that no deer wore red feathers. He pointed to the log, and the warriors behind him looked it over, but none had seen the feathers. As they passed by the log's location, Francois never took his eyes off it. He did not trust these woods, and he did not care that he didn't. Something was brewing, and the culmination of the suspense was very near.

It came at another bend in the trail, when the trail split two medium-sized pines that had grown close together. Francois did not see anything on the other side, but when he came out of the pines, he felt the whoosh of wind as an arrow flew within inches of his scalp. His spine tingled at the close call, but his body moved into reflex mode. He stepped behind the trunk of a large oak that sat just off of the trail and scanned the brush where the arrow had come from. His eyes detected nothing as he finished loading his gun.

Looking back, Francois jumped with surprise to see none of the Senecas. They had all disappeared into the woods around him, and he was the lone human standing up. *Easy target,* he thought to himself as he crouched down so as to disappear from view. When he reached the ground, he crawled along for about a dozen feet so that any arrows shot at his last-seen position would be clean misses. Indians were good shots, and he did not want any closer calls than the one he had already survived. That was plenty for one day.

The world was still, and Francois felt sweat trickle down his neck and arms. It tickled him, but he dared not move to rub it. Movement might give his position away, and he did not want to be seen first. He was breathing heavily, and he feared that it would give away his position, but no one stirred out in the forest. In fact, nothing stirred. No man, beast, or plant dared move—as if the life of the very world itself were hanging in the balance. The forest was one giant mass of silence, as if it were a picture that Francois were looking at in the French castle at Fort Niagara. It was prettier than a painting on a wall, but it was also deadlier than a hurricane at sea.

Francois was so tense that his muscles were sore. He was lying on his stomach, but his knees and elbows were ready to spring his body up if the need arose. His eyes were peeled, and he dared not blink, but it did him no good. He still couldn't see his friends or enemies. Maybe they had left him. He dearly hoped not, but he knew that it could be so. Indians were not loyal to comrades in the same way that Europeans were. They had respect for their fellow man and were good at working in teams, but there was something that Europeans had that the Indians didn't, and Francois worried that he had been left alone to face the Mohawks. Of course, there were scalps to take here, so there was a good chance that the Senecas were still around just biding their time. If so, then Francois was disappointed by their biding: he had never been a very patient person.

Suddenly—movement. An Indian was crawling along in a slight gully right in front of Francois, but it was moving away from him. Francois started to lift his musket, but now he had to figure out one very important question: how do you tell the difference between a Mohawk and a Seneca?

The Indian was moving slowly, and every ten or so-seconds, it would stop and glance to the right where the trail was. This suggested that this Indian was Mohawk, but Francois did not want to find out by shooting it and then observing which group cheered and which group howled. Precaution was still his best hope for survival, so Francois kept the gun leveled on the Indian, ready to fire if the opportunity struck.

"Whaoooooaaaaaooooo!" The Indian yell echoed through the woods. It came from Francois's right, and he turned to see an almost-naked Indian leap at another Indian who was lying behind a log. As that Indian stood up to fight, Francois recognized it as the Indian who had been behind him in the line, the one who had started to draw his bow when Francois had first met the group. As the two came together, Francois saw the viciousness of their knife cuts as they slashed at each other's bodies. Both took some blows, but the Seneca took more. As the Mohawk raised his knife to bring down on the Seneca's head, Francois turned his musket and took aim. The knife blow missed, but the Mohawk's knife was instantly coming back up, thrusting straight for the heart. Francois prayed that he would not jerk his muzzle when he fired, and with an extremely slight hesitation, he squeezed the trigger. The fire blazed out of the barrel like a roaring lion's breath, and just an instant later, the sound of the shot echoed through the woods. Francois stared through the smoke, but it was too thick to see anything. As it gradually cleared, however, he saw one Indian standing, and the other one lying at its feet. After a few more seconds, he saw that the Mohawk was the one on the ground, and the Seneca was the one standing. It held the Mohawk's scalp over its head and let out one long loud yell.

"Whaaooooooaaaaaeeeee!"

Francois did not know if he had shot the Mohawk or not, but he was glad that the Mohawk was the one down. This was no time for glory, however, as his position was now known by every Indian in the forest.

The Seneca looked over at him. He raised his hand in greeting and then began to look around. Francois pointed to the gully where he had seen the Indian. It was gone now, which suggested that it was a Mohawk.

"One Indian crawled through that gully. I do not know where it went."

The Seneca scanned the area where Francois pointed. He didn't see it, either. He took one step forward, then looked back at Francois. He started to say something, but then his eyes grew wide, and he shouted, "Look out!"

Francois didn't think. He didn't react. He didn't even startle. He just rolled. Almost immediately after he did he heard a tomahawk strike something and knew that it was supposed to have hit his back. He did not think on this very long, however, as there was not time for that. After several rolls, he jumped up and started running. After he had gone about a dozen yards, he dove back down to the ground. An arrow hit a tree above him, right where his head had been not two seconds before. Knowing that he had better find a new position, Francois crawled a few more yards away. Sitting up into a crouch, he studied his surroundings, breathing heavily. The Indian who had tried to kill him had not seen where he went, but his search was bringing him closer. Another Indian had appeared about ten yards away, but this one was also unaware of Francois's location. Off in the woods somewhere, a scream went out, and Francois knew that another brave had been killed, though he did not know the tribal allegiance. He hoped it was a Mohawk who had been killed, but he knew there was a good chance that it was a Seneca.

The Indian who had tried to tomahawk Francois now saw him and was coming through the brush faster than Francois could think. He did not have time to load his musket, but his knife was ready at hand. Drawing it from its sheath, he threw it at the oncoming warrior. The warrior's facial expression did not change as the knife hit him right in the chest. As the blade sank into his heart, he started to stumble. Blood started to run, and then the warrior fell headlong into the ferns and moss that covered the forest floor. Francois stared at the dead man for only an instant, then turned on the other warrior who was coming at a canter almost as fast as a horse's. Francois did not even have time to draw his tomahawk, so he didn't. Instead, as the Indian drew near, Francois lifted the stock of his musket to meet it.

As the Indian jumped at Francois, knife in hand, Francois swung his cudgel. The blow caught the Indian full in the face, and the bone in the nose shattered. Blood was everywhere, including on Francois, and the Indian fell down much the same as his comrade had—headlong into the ferns and moss. Francois glimpsed movement out of the corner of his eye, but when he turned, gun poised for another swing, he saw that it was one of the Senecas. The others came out of the brush, two slightly injured. One had been killed, but the Mohawk assassin had not survived, either. All six Mohawks had been killed, and the Indians were now scalping the bodies. Francois's heart was still returning to its normal pace, but he felt very good about the battle he had just fought. He had killed three very fierce warriors and had not a scratch to show for it.

After the Indians had taken their scalps, they began to take valuables from the bodies. There weren't many things that the Indians wanted since they already had most of the items, but Francois found many things that he did not have. He took a knife off the warrior he had thrown his knife into, bringing his total to two. He also took the bow and quiver of arrows off the Indian he had shot, adding these to his personal arsenal. He decided to practice with the bow and arrows much, as their ammunition could be made from the forest. Guns needed lead and gunpowder, which had to be bought or traded for at one of the forts. If he was ever in a situation where survival depended on living off the wilderness, then he had a better chance of surviving with a bow and arrows. Thus the ability to use them could be a very important skill. This thought coupled with the excitement of surviving his first battle occupied Francois's mind as the Seneca party once again headed off, single file, down the old trail in the woods.

8

THE FIRE SHINED brightly, casting glows around the camp. As the three men around it ate silently of their venison jerky, the owls in the distance hooted their night calls, telling of hares and mice scurrying below them. A long time after the men had finished their supper, one of them broke the silence.

"Been thinkin'," he said, "and I wonder how Francois is doing back at Fort Niagara. He has the makin's to be a fine voyageur, and I sure hope that he will wait for us to return. However, I don't picture that he'll wait around at the fort too long. *Non, monsieur,* he'll head off into the woods to explore and learn. That is why he will be a good voyageur. Not because of his paddling ability, though that is needed, but because of his curiosity. He is a pupil of nature, and nature will teach him much. I do like that lad. He will be a great man someday."

"Perhaps," one of his companions replied, "though I do believe that he has a level of naivete that will one day kill him. Francois is just a lad from the city who will fall like all city folks do—hard. You think too highly of him, Alexandre. He is not really all that special."

"I cannot agree with you on that, Pierre," Alexandre thoughtfully replied. "For Francois will not allow himself to be elevated above nature or death. Many men have died because of their pride, and Francois has an attitude that will not allow his pride to take hold. *Non*, Pierre, I assure you that he will be one of the greatest men to walk this land, and someday, I, Alexandre Durand, will be proud to say that I knew Francois. I gave him his start and am looking forward to seeing where he finishes."

"You are so ridiculous, Alexandre. Francois will never be any of the things you say. You are more naive than you realize, and you are thought to be the best voyageur in New France! Francois will never make it in this wilderness. He comes from the city."

"May I point out that you are also from the city, Pierre," the third companion stated matter-of-factly, "and that you were extremely clumsy and naive when you first arrived in this wilderness. Many years' experience has turned you into a real backwoodsman, however, and I do believe that a few years will make Francois one as well. This land is not for lazy men, and I do not believe Francois to be lazy."

Pierre had lost. He gave Eugene, the last speaker, a very dirty look, then rolled under his blankets to turn his back to the fire and his companions. Alexandre and Eugene each exchanged slight smiles, then huddled under their blankets as well. The evening air was already chilly, and the temperature was more than likely to drop more before dawn arrived.

Meanwhile, several hundred miles and one great lake away, Francois also lay facing a campfire. His Seneca companions were all lying around it as well, except for the one on guard. They did not expect pursuit or attack, but one must never be too careful in these woods; the events of the afternoon had proved this to be a fact.

As Francois thought back on the skirmish of the afternoon, he slowly began to realize how many close calls he had survived. When he was fighting, he had not been focused on his chances; he had had other more important things to worry about. Now, thinking back, he realized that God had saved him from the scalp-thirsty Mohawk warriors. No other possibility existed. Francois shivered when he remembered the Indian who had tried to tomahawk him in the back while he was lying down. That had been the closest call, and the memory brought sweat to the pores of his skin. He quickly came to his senses and admonished himself for perspiring on such a cool night. Then, yawning with exhaustion, he turned away from the fire and went to sleep.

It was the sun that woke him. Though the trees blocked most of the glare, there were many small patches of sunlight on the forest floor. Francois glanced around quickly and noticed that three of the Indians were already up, one preparing some corn cakes for breakfast.

"Here," Francois said as he offered the last of his deer meat for the meal.

The Indian grunted and nodded his approval, and Francois knew that his contribution would be appreciated. The Senecas, in their haste to return to their village before the Mohawks, had not hunted recently. Francois stretched his aching body to relieve some of the stiffness and then put on his fringed buckskin jacket. Gathering up his weapons and haversack, he was ready to move out whenever the Indians were. But first, breakfast.

Francois had no idea how far he traveled that day, or exactly where he was at the day's end, but he knew that a lot of ground had been traveled. The Indians had been pushing their pace a bit, and Francois knew that the confrontation with the Mohawks had prolonged the trip, and they were eager to return to their village. The Mohawk event had made them anxious as well.

As Francois lay down at the fire that night, he thought back on all of the sights he had seen that day. Many large trees, many small trees, bogs, meadows, ponds, and wildlife of all kinds had been seen throughout the day's travels. There had been some mountains that they had traversed, and Francois had seen many beautiful gorges as they both ascended and descended steep rocky slopes. The woodlands were thick on these mountains as well as in the lowlands, which screened the movements of the party as they traveled on, pressing toward the Seneca village. The pace had really exhausted Francois, and as he sat and reminisced, he subconsciously fell asleep.

At about noon on the next day, the group worked their way across a mountainside forest, still following the same trail they had started out on. It had become hard to follow in spots, but if one looked carefully enough, it could still be found. The stream they had been following all morning was currently flowing at the base of the mountain, but the gurgle of its water rippling over the rocks on the streambed could still be heard over the other sounds of the forest. Somewhere nearby a bird chirped, off in the distance a deer dashed through the woods; but nothing drowned out the sound of the steadily rippling stream.

As the trail circled around the mountain, the group came to a small clearing. They were now on a small rocky plateau, looking over a beautifully wooded valley before them. Off to the left, at the east side of the valley, the stream that the group had been following ran as steady as ever. A decent-sized Indian village was located on the stream's west bank, and many Indians were milling about, doing various tasks. At the southern end of the village, a small group of hunters returned with game for the day's big meal. Several Indian girls and young women were gathering water at the stream, and several boys were taking target practice in a small archery range at the village's north end.

As the party approached the village, Francois felt butterflies in his stomach. He did not know how he would be welcomed, and he was not sure how long he was expected to stay. All he knew was that he would not stay long if any arrows, knives, or tomahawks came within two feet of his scalp. He had had enough close calls on this trip.

As the Indians walked into the village, one of the warriors gave a whoop to announce their presence. At the call, many of the women and children looked up from their tasks, and several family members came running to greet the returning men. The family of the fallen brave mourned their share for the loss, but the five joyful families prevented gloom from striking the whole tribe. Throughout this whole ordeal, Francois had hung back away from the group, and no one had noticed him yet.

As the Indians showed off their scalps, however, one of the late-arriving teenage girls noticed Francois and made a strange noise of curiosity before exclaiming a few sentences in the Seneca tongue. Francois did not know what she said or meant, but the whole village was looking at him now. Francois felt the blood rush to his head and wished that he could just disappear, until the leader of the raiding party stepped forward and introduced him to the rest of the tribe. After a small conversation that Francois did not understand, the leader turned to Francois and spoke in a mix of French and Seneca, just enough of each so that both Francois and the tribe could understand his words. He told about Francois's brave actions in the fight against the Mohawks, and Francois felt his cheeks flushing again. After some more conversation among the Senecas, the leader turned to Francois and proudly announced, "The tribe thanks Francois for defending their warriors against our Mohawk enemies and is impressed by your bravery. Wherever your travels take you, know that you will always have friends in our village."

The cheer that rose up was enough to make Francois turn even redder, if that was possible. As he walked through the village at the chief's side, he noticed many young people his age staring at him. He tried not to focus on anyone in particular, but their looks verified what he was afraid of: he was in a position of honor that many of the young warriors around him coveted. He could see the longing and jealousy in their faces and knew that many had worked hard for just such an opportunity. He also noticed that more girls were looking at him, probably because of his position in relation to the chief; and the looks that they gave him made Francois more uncomfortable than the looks of the young men did. Francois knew that he could not escape the village without being rude, so he decided to bear the embarrassment as best he could and then leave at the first opportunity. If God and Francois agreed on timing, then that opportunity would come really soon.

9

Francois awoke slowly, then nearly jumped up with horror when he saw the furs and people who surrounded him. It took only a second to remember where he was and why, and then he began to calm down.

He was inside of a long bark-covered hut that was built on a timber frame. There were many families that shared the building, and each family quarters was separated from the others by deer or bear skins. Francois had slept the night on a wooden cot-like contraption, but many of the Indians had slept on the floor. The air inside was stuffy and smelled of the smoke and meat of days past. Francois didn't much like the smells or humidity level, but the hut had a homey feel that he had catered to immediately.

As the other Indians woke up and began their daily tasks, Francois found himself sitting idly in a corner. Even there, he found himself constantly in the way. He did not like being a nuisance to his companions, but he did not know what the tribe would think if he left and took a walk through the village. It might be helpful, but it might also seem rude to them; Francois didn't know them well enough. Time would cure that, he reasoned, so he tried to learn as he observed the Indians moving quickly from daily habit, speaking rapidly in a foreign language.

One of the adult women in the longhouse who appeared to be about forty years old turned to Francois and told him something in her language that he did not have the least chance of understanding. The blood began to creep into his cheeks as he ashamedly shook his head, communicating that he couldn't understand her tongue. She did not seem the least bit upset about it and turned to one of the other women there. She repeated her message, and then the other woman turned to Francois with a warm smile and said, "Brown Rabbit needs more meat for breakfast and wonders if you would go hunt for some. Her son, Running Deer, would be glad to accompany you to show you the best sites in the valley." Francois nodded dumbly, glad for something to do, and reached for his musket and shot bag. Following the young warrior who stepped forward, the two men headed out into the morning sunshine to provide for the day's first meal.

Running Deer could not speak much French, but he knew enough words to make a point to Francois when necessary. Francois found himself recognizing a few words from Running Deer as well and was glad to start learning what they meant. By the time the two had returned to the village with a rabbit and two turkeys, Francois knew the Indian words for *deer*, *rabbit*, *turkey*, *tree*, and *hunt*. He was very pleased with his progress and was even more pleased by the fact that Running Deer was impressed by his quick mind. It gave Francois a new measure of self-assurance and confidence as he began to make friends with the natives.

After breakfast, Running Deer took Francois out to the archery range on the northern outskirts of the village. Francois had improved much since he had picked up the weapons off the Mohawk, but the never-ending travel of the group had prevented him from practicing a lot. Now he found that Running Deer's supervision was very helpful, and he learned several tips from the more experienced marksman that he never would have figured out on his own. By the end of the morning, he had already hit the center of the target three times.

At noon or thereabouts, Francois and Running Deer headed to the stream to fish. Running Deer had just made a new fishing spear, and he was anxious to try it out. Francois watched intently as Running Deer looked the stream over, looking for shady spots that fish might be hiding in. He waited with a patience that amazed even Francois, and still no fish had come. Francois was ready to give up. Running Deer was close. Then it came. A large brook trout swam out into the sunshine just enough, and Running Deer's spear flashed. Francois could not believe his eyes. The spear had been thrown so quickly like lightning, and the trout was now being held in Running Deer's hands, dead. Francois felt a surge of excitement go through him and gladly accepted the spear to try his own hand. The sense of boredom had left him, and he was intent on catching his own fish. He waited for only a few minutes before a fish appeared out of the shadows. The spear flashed through the water, but the throw differed from Running Deer's in two ways: the spear was not thrown nearly as hard, and this time it missed its target. Disappointment hit Francois full force, but Running Deer's encouraging remarks quickly made his spirits lighten. He settled in again, but this time his previous failure gave him determination. He had to wait longer this time as the fish were not trusting for several minutes, but when the next fish ventured out of the darkness, Francois was ready for it. He threw his spear with as much force as he could muster, but this shot also missed. Francois was again disappointed, but Running Deer's encouragement again prevented Francois's spirits from staying down. He was ready to try again.

They moved a little farther downstream as Running Deer feared the fish would not venture forth in the previous hole. When they reached another one farther to the north, Francois again began to probe the waters with his eyes searching for fish. When one did finally swim forth,

Francois threw the spear with more force than he had his previous two. After the splash, Francois drew the spear out to see if he had hit his target, but Running Deer was already celebrating. He jumped up and down wildly, and when Francois saw the large brook trout on the spearhead, he began to jump up and down too. Running Deer then showed him how to kill the fish, and they started off to the village together. They gave the two fish to Running Deer's mother, who complimented and marveled appropriately, and then ran off into the woods with grins on both of their faces. They had only met each other that morning, but they were already the best of friends having adventures together. And the day wasn't even over yet.

Francois spent more days at the village than he had planned to, and the Indians did not seem to mind at all. Running Deer was like the brother that Francois never had, and Brown Rabbit, Running Deer's mother, was like the mother that Francois was missing. Francois greatly improved his archery skills, as well as his use of the knife and tomahawk. He had learned how to fish and how to prepare a caught fish for food, and he had made friends who would be his forever. Still, the holes that Running Deer and Brown Rabbit filled made him remember what he had left behind in France. He again thought about his family, wondered how they were doing, and felt a sad flood of emotions wash over him. He missed them. Not the life he would have had to live in France, but he missed his family.

When Francois chose to leave the village, the whole tribe turned out to see him go. The chief once again thanked him for his bravery against their Mohawk enemies, and the warriors all came out to him to express thanks and comradeship. Francois knew that he would miss these people, but his emotions were such as required him to leave. Besides, winter was coming, and he wanted to be with his own people when it arrived. He planned to come back, though he did not know when he would. Right now, he had to reach Fort Niagara before Alexandre did and get a ride back to Montreal—he was going to be a voyageur.

10

Francois was walking through the woods several days later when he came upon a small garden plot. Surprised, he went into it to get a closer look. There were only a few plants left, as the season was almost over, and those that remained appeared to be dead from the frost of the night before.

The days had been much colder now, along with the nights. The last few mornings Francois had awoken to frost on the ground, but the sun had always warmed the world when it appeared. Now, today, the sun was shining brightly, and the temperature was still very cool. Francois was glad that he was near the safety and warmth of the fort.

A movement in the brush across the plot startled Francois. He began to reach for his gun then thought better of it. It would take too long to load. Instead, he grabbed his knife out of its sheath and prepared to defend himself. Whatever was in the woods did not seem to be aware of Francois's presence, as it kept on walking toward the clearing. Francois was ready, though a little anxious, as he did not know what type of enemy he could meet here. He was, after all, only half a mile or so from the fort itself. What enemy would be bold enough to come that close to the fort? Then Francois had a sickening thought. What if the fort has been taken? What would he do then?

His thoughts were interrupted by the appearance of a man at the edge of the clearing. The man was obviously French, and he was wearing a shirt, vest, and military pants, but he was not wearing his coat. Francois was still recovering from the relief of seeing a fellow countryman when the soldier spoke.

"Francois?"

Francois, startled, looked more closely at the man's face. "Bertrand!" he yelled.

The two ran to each other to embrace, and then they were both talking excitedly, telling each other of everything that had happened to each of them in the past weeks. Bertrand had grown a thick beard, which is why Francois had not recognized him. As the two headed off to the fort, Francois asked Bertrand if Alexandre had arrived yet.

"Not yet," Bertrand replied with satisfaction, "but I expect him to show up any day now. Alexandre never was one to travel when the snow was flying. Not that he couldn't, of course, but the risks are too great for even Alexandre to take. He is more cunning than that."

Francois was relieved that he had not missed his ride back to Montreal.

Word of Francois's arrival spread quickly. Many Indians from the lower village came shyly to Francois to ask how their Indian brothers and sisters were faring. Francois gave each one a detailed report, though the story became less and less detailed each time he told it. He told of his fight, though he tried to keep himself out of it, at least the parts that made him seem like a brave warrior. Not that he wouldn't mind them hearing it, but he felt uncomfortable boasting about his own valor.

Many of the soldiers asked Francois about his travels as well. Most were interested in what he ate and did while at the Indian village, but many wanted to hear about the battle or the specific characters of the different Indians he had encountered. Francois had to tell the different stories so many times over his first few days back at the fort that he came to wish he had never left the fort in the first place. If he could have been paid to tell his tales, he knew that he would have been the richest man in New France.

Two weeks after Francois arrived, Alexandre did. Francois had been everywhere that morning, visiting the baker and talking with both Alphonse and Bertrand before taking his musket to the gunsmith to have it repaired. He had been out hunting the day before and had noticed that the hammer mechanism was not working as it should.

"I hear that you had some mighty interesting travels recently, lad." The gunsmith kindly noted with a twinkle in his eye. "But I am afraid the stories that have reached me are not much more than rumors. Therefore, I would like to hear all about it firsthand."

Francois began his now-boring tale, recalling the events of the past month or two for the hundredth time, while the gunsmith skillfully fixed the hammer mechanism on the musket. When he was done, Francois thanked him kindly and paid him for his efforts. As he stepped out of the smith's cabin, he turned toward the river. He gazed at the opposite bank for a minute or two, then gazed out onto the lake. Soon he hoped to be canoeing on that lake headed for Montreal, where he would winter over. Everything was planned out, but first Alexandre had to come.

The day was milder than the previous week or so had been, and the sun was shining, so Francois decided to take a canoe out onto the river. It had been awhile since he had practiced, and he longed to be paddling again. Soon he would be doing it every day for several weeks, and he knew that the novelty would wear off then. It was for this reason that he went out now to enjoy the feeling of gliding through the water by his own muscle power.

Francois started by heading into Lake Ontario. It was a bit choppy, so he did not stay long, but he wanted to get a feel for the lake's waves. After he had tried them out a bit, he headed up the Niagara River. It was not easy going, but he managed to make steady progress; and in no time at all he was well past the fort and continuing on. It was at a point about three-quarters of a mile from the lower village where Francois first saw the two canoes.

They were coming quickly toward him, which was only possible because they were paddling downriver, and the movements of the boats told that they were manned by professional paddlers. Francois hoped that it was Alexandre, Pierre, and Eugene, but one could never be sure; many people traveled this waterway, and it could be anyone coming right now.

When the boats came nearer, however, Francois began to get a better glimpse of who was in them. Three people…all men…all French…One of them was very tall with a handlebar mustache, now very scraggly from lack of attention. One appeared middle-height with broad shoulders and thick arms. He was still too far away for Francois to make out any definite facial features, but his physique was certainly that of Alexandre. As the canoes came closer, Francois found that his suspicions were true: it *was* Alexandre. Excited beyond words, all Francois could manage to call out was "Alexandre!"

Alexandre turned, and when he saw who it was waving to him, he excitedly waved back, yelling, "Francois, Francois!"

Francois paddled faster. So did Alexandre. As the boats came nearer, both men started talking at once. Francois felt like he had been reunited with a father; Alexandre like he had been reunited with a son. In their excitement, both men forgot about Eugene and Pierre. Eugene did not mind at all, but Pierre felt a bit put off. He still did not see anything special about the buckskin-clad city boy who was enthusiastically conversing with his boss.

Francois and Alexandre certainly would have hugged had they not been in two different canoes on the Niagara River. Alexandre, good boater that he was, could probably have managed it anyway, but Francois would not have had a chance of staying upright, and they both knew it. So they decided to wait on the bear hug until all the boats were ashore.

The fort now seemed far away to Francois, but catching up with the three men made the trip seem fairly short. Eugene and Pierre were now being included in the conversation. Eugene was eager to tell of his experiences and almost as eager to hear of Francois's, but Pierre sat rather sulkily, chewing on his mustache and glowering at all three of his companions. He was not ready to forgive them for leaving him out of their excitement, and he wanted to repay them by ignoring them. His objective was not achieved, however, as they eventually just ignored him and continued conversing on their own.

The next Sunday morning, Alexandre joined Francois at the castle's chapel for the service. Francois had attended the service every Sunday since he had returned, but no one whom he knew really well went. This left him feeling lonely during the service even though he enjoyed hearing the reading of the scriptures and feeling the emotions of holy communion. The fact that Alexandre attended the chapel service every time he got a chance made Francois feel even better about associating with the simple but kind voyageur.

After the service, Francois took a walk through the woods with Bertrand, Alexandre, and Ètienne, one of Bertrand's soldier friends. After a while, Eugene joined the quartet, making them a quintet, and the group hiked even farther away from the fort. Snow had fallen a couple of days ago, but it had all melted with the milder weather of the past day or so. The sun was shining, and the woods were full of thin shadows from the leafless trees. The leaves were rustling around at the Frenchmen's feet, and the breeze blowing made the temperature seem colder than it actually was.

As the men tramped through the leaves and around the barren trees, they came to a well-worn deer trail that led into a thicket. Only Ètienne and Eugene had muskets, but Alexandre did have a pistol.

"We should be getting back to the fort," Francois remarked. "It will be getting dark soon."

"Let us at least go into the thicket and see where it leads," Eugene countered. "There will be light for at least another hour or two."

"*Oui*, that there will, lad," Alexandre began, then continued, "but I agree with Francois. The sooner we get back to the fort, the better."

"I think we should go just a *little* bit farther," Eugene replied, "just to see if there are any deer. A fresh buck would sure taste good with tonight's dinner."

"I think that we are all right for another half of an hour," Ètienne put in, "the light will stay with plenty of time for getting back."

So they started off. Bertrand had not spoken, and he did not really have an opinion either way. Francois and Alexandre both looked at each other and shrugged, but they did not argue further. They knew that the group would be safest if they all stayed together. So, with doubts crossing their minds, they joined the group now, following the deer trail.

Eugene was leading. Ètienne was right behind, followed by Bertrand, Francois, and Alexandre, in that order. Nothing seemed to be wrong in the forest, though the animal sounds had died down. The only sound came from a lone catbird somewhere to the east that was calling for its mate.

After the Frenchmen crossed a small stream, the woods thickened so that one could hardly move to the left or right from the path. On top of that, the brambles were so thick overhead that one could not stand to full height when following the trail, either. This greatly impeded Francois's ability to run as he was used to running at full height, able to take full long strides. He now hoped that they would get out of this thicket soon as it was not a desirable place to be ambushed.

As the group came out of the thicket, they found a small spring off to their right that was spewing forth fresh clear water. After kneeling to take a drink, the men debated which way to take on their return route.

"We should not return by the route we just came out of," Francois wisely advised, "it is too narrow a trail to defend should we be ambushed. We also would not be able to leave the trail, so we would be trapped in whatever position we were in when attacked."

"Right you are, lad," Alexandre encouraged, "I would sooner take a route twice that length than return by that trail. It has danger written all over it, and it does indeed place us in a very untenable position should we be ambushed by Indians."

Eugene, Ètienne, and Bertrand did not like the feel of the thicket either, so they all agreed to start back to the north of their current position until they found a trail that headed west. And so agreeing, they started out.

Francois was now in the lead. That is why he first noticed the Indians. Well, the Indians and their prisoners. They were traveling along an east-west trail, the trail that the French group would be turning onto when they reached it. Francois came up short quickly and was almost knocked down by Ètienne, who was following him a little too closely. Francois stumbled forward but did not fall. The others all stopped a few feet behind him, and the Indians all stopped and stared as well. They were Senecas, and they had obviously just returned from a raiding party. There were eight of them, and only one of those did not have any scalps hanging from his leather belt. Several had two or three.

There were also three prisoners in the group. One, a little boy, appeared to be the child of another prisoner, a woman who appeared to be about thirty-five. He clung to her skirts as if his life depended upon it, but she had been carrying him a minute before, so he had obviously been hitching a ride most of the time. The trip had been fatiguing to both of them, and both showed signs of exhaustion.

The other prisoner was a girl of about fifteen, who had obviously been really pretty before this long trip. Her hair, an attractive medium-brown, was matted from lack of attention, and her dress, once a simple calico print, was now torn and tattered in more places than could be counted. Her hands were bound in front of her, the reason being quickly explained by one of warriors: two suns ago, she had tried to escape from her captors. She had escaped the camp and drawn a chase, but the days of little nourishment and exhaustive trekking had taken their toll, and she had been easily outrun. Now she was watched more closely, and any chances of escape had completely vanished.

"She is lucky to still be alive," Alexandre murmured under his breath, loud enough for his companions to hear. Francois had not yet learned of such things, but Ètienne, Bertrand, and Eugene had, and they all knew that Alexandre was right.

The Frenchmen joined the Indian troop, and they all headed west toward Fort Niagara. The shadows were beginning to lengthen now, and the air was getting cooler, but they were not daunted. They wanted to reach the fort tonight instead of risk snow or rain falling on them out in the open.

They pushed on at a very brisk pace. It was no problem for the Indians, who had trained for such travel ever since they were seven or eight years old, or even for the voyageurs, who were used to traversing rougher terrain than this; but the prisoners had a very hard time keeping up with the painted men who dragged them along. They had been drained of most of their energy already, and a sped-up forced march at the end of a long day was not the way to recover. Still, they had no choice, so they plodded on as best they could, fearful of the consequence for straggling.

It was almost dark when they reached the fort. The guards were just starting to draw up the drawbridge to the gate of Six Nations when Alexandre called out loudly, "Hold the gate for just a minute!"

"Who is there?" came the cry from the corporal on guard.

"Alexandre, Francois, Eugene, and two off-duty soldiers," Alexandre replied, "plus eight Seneca Indians and their three captives."

Alexandre heard the low sympathetic murmur of voices and knew that the soldiers were remarking about the last group mentioned. After a slight pause, the corporal called again.

"We will let the bridge down. Come in quickly, and the commandant will see the Indians."

The bridge was let down, and the travelers marched into the fort. The Indians marched proudly, for now was their first chance to show off their spoils of war. The Frenchmen marched in casually, neither proud nor ashamed, just exhausted and ready to go to bed. The prisoners walked in with their heads down and did not even dare to look up at the interior of the fort they were in. They just kept walking straight ahead, eyes on the feet in front of them. It was in this manner that they walked into the French castle, where they were ushered into one of the dark stone-walled rooms. Each person took his or her pose and prepared for the entrance of the commandant.

As the commandant walked in, his eyes gazed over those who had assembled in the room. He noticed the five Frenchmen standing to his left, gave them a slight nod with a smile, then nodded to the eight Indians who stood glaring at him through their paint-covered faces. Then his eyes drifted to the three English prisoners, one a boy, one a worried mother, and the other a terrified teenager. The commandant saw the looks of pleading in their eyes and felt a great surge of pity go through his whole body. He turned away from them so that they would not see the tears forming in his eyes and then fought for control of his emotions. He knew that if he showed emotion or fear for these prisoners, the Indians would refuse to part with them.

They might even kill them. He knew that this must not happen and determined to do whatever he could to rescue them from their savage captors. He turned to his guests, greeted them cordially, and settled in to make conversation about their raid. The ransom had begun.

11

FRANCOIS LISTENED INTENTLY to the chatter, though he had a hard time following much of what the Indians said. Sergeant Basil acted as an interpreter, but the commandant knew much of the Seneca tongue, so he needed an interpretation only rarely. This left Francois guessing what most of the Indian words meant, and so his understanding of the whole exchange was limited.

The Indians, just as the commandant had feared, were very hesitant to let their prisoners go. Their chief had just lost his son, and the little boy would make a perfect replacement, the mother could be his nurse until he was of age, and the girl could become the wife of one of the braves in the tribe. Judging by their glances, Francois could tell that two or three of the braves in this party already had their eyes on her, and he knew there was not much chance of her staying at the fort.

As the conversation turned to other things, however, the commandant found a useful bit of bargaining information: the tribe to which these Indians belonged was very poor. They had been pushed around by other tribes, and their current location was not good for farming or furs, so they did not stand much chance of improving their situation. The village had been getting by on little food in the past few moons, some nights not having anything to eat. The commandant knew that this was his best basis for exchange and proceeded accordingly.

"We feel for our Seneca brothers and sisters who must regularly endure hunger. This war with the English will require many to continue to endure hunger. Though our brothers, the Senecas, are in want of food and clothing, here at Fort Niagara, we French have more than we need. We would be happy to supply our brothers with food and cloth for their families so that they may not go hungry during the winter ahead."

And turning to Lieutenant Rousseau, he ordered, "Bring flour and red cloth to show we mean what we say."

The Lieutenant nodded and hurried to do as bidden.

The Indians, though hungry, were not dumb. They knew that the commandant wanted their prisoners, and they knew that the tribe was counting on them bringing a new chief's son home. Still, when the soldiers arrived carrying flour and cloth—red cloth, no less—the warriors found it hard to resist an exchange. Their chief was grieving his son, but he was also hungry, and the choice was a hard one to make.

The commandant, seeing the temptation in their eyes, ordered more items from the storehouse. Knives, beads, and trinkets were procured this time, and the greed on the Indians' faces deepened.

"The Senecas shall have ten sacks of flour and four bolts of red cloth for the young maiden there." And the commandant pointed to the girl.

The Indians startled out of their reveries and began to bargain back.

"We keep for work. She very strong and healthy. One of our braves take her as squaw."

"But you told me you are hungry," the commandant politely reminded them, "and she will be one more person to feed. If you take these items, you will have more food and less people to share it."

"We keep maiden," the leader firmly announced.

"We'll throw in two blankets and some knives." The commandant offered, showing these items to the Indians. Their eyes lit up, but their faces remained stern and hard.

"We keep maiden," the leader said even more firmly than before.

The commandant sadly moved on. He had lost.

"For the woman and her son, we will give ten sacks of flour, five bolts of red cloth, and some knives," the commandant began. He knew that the boy would be worth more to them, but he wanted to start low.

"You take woman," the leader said defiantly, "but boy stay with us. He be our chief's son."

"But how will you feed your families if you don't return with food?" the commandant asked. He knew that the mother should stay with her child, and he did not plan to separate them, even if that meant they both went with the Indians.

"Our families strong. We fight through winter. We hunt and search for berries, and we will survive."

"These plans sound risky," the commandant stated, calmer than he felt. "What if there are not many berries near your village? What if the game is scarce? We will give you flour to fill your stomachs and cloth for your squaws so the winter will not be so hard. We will give your maidens beads and your young men knives. Our brothers the Senecas will be rich and powerful again like they were in the days of your ancestors. May the Seneca nation rise again to power!"

The Senecas were impressed by the words of the commandant, and their awe, along with their need for food, caused them to exchange the mother and her son for the items the commandant had offered. The commandant again tried to persuade the Indians to give up the girl, but they firmly refused. As the Indians prepared to leave, the girl realized what had not happened. As the warriors began to march single file out of the room, the girl turned to the commandant and pleadingly whispered softly under her breath, "*Sauve moi.*"

The commandant's breath caught in his throat, and he almost cried. Francois did. They both fought for control as they watched her leave with her new family.

"Will she ever be able to come home?" Francois asked shakily. He was not sure that he wanted to know the answer. It was too obvious.

"Only if she escapes, lad," Alexandre huskily replied. He knew that there was not much chance of that, but he did not mention it. He could tell that Francois already knew. Instead, he placed one hand on Francois's shoulder, and whispered, "Better get to bed. It is very late." Francois could only nod.

As he crept under his blankets in the north redoubt, Francois could not shut out the two words that the girl had whispered to the commandant before she was led away. *Sauve moi, sauve moi, sauve moi* kept running through his head, robbing him of any chance of sleep. He did not know how she had learned French, but she had known enough to break his heart. His emotions welled up inside him once again, and he could not help but cry as he tossed and turned, trying to find a comfortable position. After he had cried his eyes dry, he felt three words come into his mind. He whispered them into the darkness to see how they sounded, "I hate war."

They sounded appropriate, and Francois felt better after saying them. War was terrible. War was fatal. And, perhaps most of all, war was devastating. Francois tossed and turned for another half-hour before exhaustion finally forced him into a sound sleep.

12

"Good-bye, Alphonse." Alexandre, Francois, Eugene, and Pierre were returning to Montreal, and they were saying their last good-byes to their friends.

"Good-bye, Francois," Alphonse replied. There seemed to be nothing more to say.

"Good-bye, Bertrand," Francois continued, and Bertrand returned his farewell the same way that Alphonse did. He also did not feel that any other words were necessary or appropriate.

"I will be back in the spring, you can count on it," Francois stated with finality, "and I will look for both of you, first thing, when I arrive."

Nods from Alphonse and Bertrand affirmed that they would do the same.

As the two canoes paddled away from the lower village, the men on shore waved to those in the boats, and vice versa. When the boats had rounded the first bend in the lakeshore, however, all waving ceased. The men in the boats turned all of their attention to paddling, and the men at the fort returned to their daily duties. The voyageurs had left for another winter and would not return until spring. Until then, the fort would need to sustain itself on the goods in its storehouses. It was now an isolated outpost on the frontier, and only its ingenuity could save it if its storehouses were empty.

The paddles dipped quickly, rhythmically, and Francois felt the surge in his heart again: he was a voyageur paddling a canoe by his own muscle power. It never ceased to amaze Francois that this feeling existed, and he once again found himself thanking God for sending Alexandre to Quebec many months before, when Francois himself had been greener than the foliage blanketing the ground. Now here they were in the same canoe, Francois dipping his paddle almost as fast and with almost as much strength as Alexandre did. Time and hard work: those were the ingredients that had made Francois the self-sustaining man that he now was, and he owed infinite debts to Alexandre for the knowledge and skills learned along the way.

As the paddles dipped and the shorebirds sang, a song slowly rose from the two canoes. Thinking back, no one really knew who started it; it was just suddenly being sung by them all. The time passed quickly for the men from France as the words and tune floated slowly, surely over the lake:

Par un dimanche au soir, M'en allant promener,
Et moi et puis François, tous deux de compagnie,
Chez le bonhomm' Gauthier on est allé veiller,
Je vais vous raconter l'tour qui m'est arrivé.

> Youpe! Youpe! sur la riviére,
> Vous ne m'entendez guére,
> Youpe! Youpe! sur la riviére,
> Vous ne m'entendez pas.

13

THREE INCHES OF snow covered the ground, and more was lightly falling from the sky when two canoes paddled up to the *quai* at Montreal. The sun had already set over the western horizon, and the voyageurs who had just arrived had completed their journey by moonlight.

Francois shivered from the cold then turned to help his three companions haul their boats ashore. When this had been done, they began to unload their boats of their cargoes. There was not much, only the personal belongings of the voyageurs themselves, so that task did not take long to complete. The voyageurs then found themselves a small clearing near the *quai* where they could set up camp for the night. They would enter the city on the morrow.

The sun shined brightly before Francois stirred. Alexandre had already been up for an hour or two, Eugene not much less, and Pierre was not even in the camp. Upon his awakening, he had chosen to head into the city right away so that he would not miss one minute of the shopping. He had money to spend.

After eating a normal breakfast of corn porridge, Francois, Alexandre, and Eugene headed into Montreal together. Francois could not believe how different the city appeared to him compared to the first time he had seen it. Oh, nothing in the city had really changed, but when Francois had walked these streets back in August, he was a pauper boy fresh from the city. This city had appeared rough and rowdy, though much of it was not unlike the slums of Paris that Francois had been used to. Still, the city's inhabitants, coupled with the woods and Indians that surrounded it, had made Francois feel like he had left civilization for good. Now, returning fresh from a three-month trek through the wilderness, this city looked like Paris itself to Francois. Its proper ladies in fancy dresses; its well-mannered, educated gentlemen wearing coats and shoes; and its straight streets lined with all types of shops equalled civility itself to the rough-clad voyageur. He found himself drinking it all in as he walked down the wooden boardwalk with his companions.

"Say, look at those tomahawks, Alexandre," Francois admired. "Those are so fancy that I would not even want to use them!"

"I agree with you, lad," Alexandre replied with his usual burst of energy. "They look much nicer than my old iron head, but my tomahawk has never let me down when I needed to get a job done. Best leave the fancy city tools in the fancy city!"

Eugene, meanwhile, was admiring one of the gold-pocket watches located in the same store.

"Sure does look pretty enough," he remarked with a sly tone, "but I would not want to chance it getting wet whilst paddling."

Francois could not help but smile at Eugene's remark, but he knew it to be true. The watch would not be worth the extra effort to keep it safe.

"Say, lads," Alexandre piped up, "this store sure does like their gold materials, don't they? The tomahawks have gold or beads on their handles and heads, the watches are all pure gold, and many of the trinkets and necklaces for the womenfolk are gold as well. Whew! Makes one wonder how this wilderness can go from rough men to European civilization so quickly. Remarkable!"

Francois felt that he had had enough of this store, and he was relieved to find that his companions felt the same. Fed up with all of the gold frivolities that this store contained, the three men stepped out into the sunshine together and walked on to the next shop.

That evening, as the men fingered and admired the items that had been purchased that day, Francois spoke up about their winter plans.

"Which tavern are we going to spend the winter in, Alexandre? I do not have much money, so I cannot stay in one that is very expensive. Do either of you know of a good but inexpensive tavern?"

Francois did not know why Alexandre and Eugene were laughing so hard, but it was obvious by the way they were letting on that he had said something humorous. He waited for them to settle down, and then he decided to get on with the conversation.

"What did I say that was so funny?" he asked. That just made them laugh harder.

"Did you really think…" Alexandre started and then lost himself in another fit of laughter. Eugene was laughing too hard to say anything, and he did not even try. Francois was starting to get a little annoyed by their joke, and Alexandre sensed his frustration. So, forcing himself back under control, he decided to explain the reason for their laughter.

"Did you really think that we were going to spend the winter in Montreal" he asked, incredulous, "in a tavern?"

Francois could not answer. What else were they planning to do?

"I am going to go on a winter trapping trip," Alexandre explained. "There are many beavers that can be trapped in the winter, up to the north, and I am going to go up there, hole up in a cabin, and trap until the spring thaw. Then I'll come down here and resume my *métier* as a voyageur."

Francois could not believe his ears. He had many questions to ask, many statements to say, but all he could manage to blurt out was, "Oh."

Eugene, still amused by the whole discussion of the past few minutes, could not contain himself any longer. "You really thought that we were going to stay here in Montreal? All winter? Do you think we would *survive* that?"

Francois started to say something smart but then checked himself. Now it made sense. What had he been thinking? That Alexandre and Eugene and Pierre were going to stay shut up in a tavern for three months? Eugene was right; could they survive that? Suddenly, without warning, the whole thing seemed really hilarious to Francois, and before he could stop himself, he was laughing harder than he had ever laughed in his life. As he rolled on the ground, holding his sides to keep them from aching, it was Eugene's and Alexandre's turn to be confused. The conversation had switched very abruptly, and now they were trying to figure out what *they* had said that was so funny. Francois explained it for them between fits of laughter and gulps of air. "I… thought…you would stay…here in Montreal…all winter!" He laughed.

Confusion reigned in Alexandre's and Eugene's minds for just a split second longer, and then the humor dawned on them too. They glanced at each other, and then, without warning, all three of them were laughing hysterically, rolling on the ground with their hands gripping their sides. As they all shared their joke of the past five or ten minutes, a renewed sense of camaraderie settled over them. These three men were being bound together by friendship, and the ties they were binding were not the kind that can be easily broken. They were lifelong ties, and these men were the kind of men it took to use such ties to claim a territory and make it a country. These men were frontiersmen, trappers, and voyageurs; *oui*, but they were also a nation's countrymen. Countrymen who would give it all to tame a land. Men who found a lonely, rough, and dangerous lifestyle to be worth the freedom that such a life gave, the fulfillment that such a life promised, and the nation that such a life brought. These men were ready to tame the wilderness individually, but they were smart enough to know that it would take all of them together to actually accomplish it. That is why they built their friendships. That is why they worked to know each other so well. That is why they shared jokes around the campfire.

The men tried to talk several times, but it never worked. Whoever started to say something always lost himself in another fit of laughter. They went on like this for a good twenty minutes before they recovered enough to converse as normal.

"So, Francois, why did you buy yourself a pocket watch? Did you really want to keep track of time?"

"Well, not necessarily, but I might as well keep track of time while I have it. We have been laughing for about eighteen minutes, though the discussion started about twenty-four minutes ago and some seconds."

Slight chuckles came from the other two party members.

"So Francois," it was Alexandre this time, "if you did not buy a watch out of desperation to keep track of time, what did you buy it for?"

Francois sobered. Should he tell them? How much? He debated for an instant, then decided to tell them all.

"Well," he began, "I bought this watch because it reminded me of my father's. He had a beautiful pocket watch back when I was five or six years old, and it had been a gift from his grandfather, whom I never knew. My father loved that watch more than anything, or so I used to think. Then, when I was about seven, my father had to close down the shop that he owned because of low sales and high taxes. He had some money left, but not much, and what he had he used as best he could to keep us clothed and fed.

"When I was about eight or nine, we had run out of money and options. Father kept looking desperately for a job, but he could not find anything. Many shops were closing down, just like father's had. There were no jobs to be found in our whole section of the city. Then the day came when father was offered a decent amount of money for his grandfather's watch. I just knew that father would turn the man down and explain that it was a family heirloom. Great was my surprise when, without hesitating or flinching, father sold the man the watch for the price offered. I wanted to tell father to refrain from the exchange, but it was all over before I knew it. I started to cry, but father told me not to. He said that there are some things in this life that are not as important as others. 'Your sisters and mother need food. You yourself need food, son. I cannot keep that watch when its sale provides much-needed nourishment for my family. Someday, you too will understand this feeling. Until then, you need to trust that I just did the right thing.'

"I did not forgive him for months even though I was grateful for the food. I do not know if he missed the watch or not, though sometimes I would catch him feeling his vest pocket as if to console himself of its absence. Or maybe it was to comfort himself by reminding him of the days when it had been present. Eventually, the money from the watch ran out, and we were forced to move to a small apartment in the slums of the city, which we were never able to leave. My family was still living there when I left."

Silence reigned around the campfire. No one dared interrupt the somber, depressing feeling that had settled in the hearts and minds of all three companions.

"And so," Francois began on a lighter note, "when I saw this watch today and remembered the one just like it that my father had proudly carried, I just had to buy it. It may be a frivolity or a useless trinket, but it is more than a watch to me. It is a memory also."

"What were your circumstances before your father's shop closed?" Alexandre asked.

"We were not gentry, but we got by just fine. Father used to say that the middle class of a country is always the strongest class, and I guess that I agree."

"So then, Francois," Eugene piped up with a mischievous smile on his face, "why did you buy the mug?"

"Because I don't have one, and it is hard to drink coffee with either my hands or my hat," Francois responded with a chuckle.

"I wondered if it was just because of the belle who was standing at the counter waiting for your money," Eugene remarked with a twinkling eye.

Alexandre laughed out loud. It was fun to watch his boys pick on each other.

"I can honestly say that I didn't really pay attention to the so-called belle at the counter," Francois defended, trying to keep the color from his cheeks and the fluster out of his mouth. "I decided that I wanted to have a mug, and since I had the money and a mug for sale in front of me, I bought one."

Eugene chuckled. "Seems to me you'll be returning to that store to shop extremely often, at least as often as you come to Montreal. That belle was sure giving you her attention."

Francois threw a blanket at Eugene, and then they both started laughing. Alexandre was still laughing, and now all three of them were again rolling on the ground together.

"So that's why you wanted to stay in a tavern in Montreal!" Eugene yelled above the uproar. That just caused more laughter around the circle. Francois's eyes were watery as he tried to gain control of himself, but then he looked at his two companions across the campfire, and he couldn't keep the laughter inside. He lost it again, and the three of them continued laughing over their good jokes of the evening.

It was this scene that Pierre found when he walked into the camp a few minutes later. He was a little tipsy from the rum he had been drinking, and he didn't care to find out what had gotten the men so stuck in laughter.

Must have tried some rum, he thought to himself as he lay down under his deerskin blanket, *and they tried to tell me to keep away from it!*

His head had barely touched the ground before he was asleep.

14

"Wow, WHAT A snug cabin!" Francois exclaimed.

Alexandre smiled. "She's a belle, all right. This cabin has kept me warm ever since I built it over five years ago. I come here every winter to trap furs, and I can honestly say that I wouldn't have it any other way."

The four men floundered through the deep snow to the cabin door, and then they took off their snowshoes before they went inside. Francois found the cabin to be just as snug inside as it was outside, though the inside was much dirtier. This could primarily be attributed to the dirt floor, but the mud chinking in the walls didn't help any, and the mud and stone fireplace and chimney completed the cabin's dirt construction. It had been built with cheap materials, Francois noted, but it had been built as solidly as nature would allow, and, as Francois also noted with satisfaction, this meant that the cabin he was currently standing in was much stronger than most of the buildings he had ever seen in France, Montreal, or Quebec. Yes, it was also stronger than the Seneca longhouses that he had lived in almost two months ago. He turned to his companions who were busy placing their bundles in certain parts of the room, and he set about to copy their actions. Each man took a corner to use as his own personal space, and Francois's corner was the one located at the front left of the cabin. Alexandre was setting up in the back left, next to the fireplace; Pierre was busy in the back right; and Eugene's corner was the front right one, though he was currently out collecting some firewood to get a blaze started.

Francois arranged his pouches how he liked them but didn't set up his bedding yet. Instead, he grabbed an iron bucket by the hearth and went outside to collect some snow. When Eugene got a fire going, it would melt the snow into water, and the men could use that for their supper.

Eugene quickly found enough wood to get a fire going, but it would take much more to keep it going. Alexandre had a large stack of kindling set at the front of the cabin to the left of the door, but all four men agreed without speaking that this stack would be saved for use during the winter storms that were sure to come. Instead, they traversed through the woods to find some large logs, and these were rolled to the clearing in which the cabin was situated and cut into appropriate lengths. Pierre and Francois worked at this while Eugene started the fire, and Alexandre took his musket and headed out to find game for the evening meal. All four were hungry as they had traveled an extra three miles today just because they were that close. This left them ready for a hot meal, but it required some very hard work beforehand.

Alexandre didn't take long in finding a brace of turkeys, and upon his return to the camp, he immediately set to work plucking feathers. When this was completed, he headed inside to prepare it over Eugene's fire, and Francois and Pierre took some extra firewood in at the same time. By the time Alexandre had those birds ready for feasting, there was a good stack of wood to the right of the door, and all four men could hear their stomachs growling above the noise of their jokes and laughter. They all sat down on the dirt floor to eat, and the mealtime conversation was nonexistent until each man had emptied his first plate. Once their plates had been refilled, however, talk began, and the men began to discuss their situation. Outside, the wind howled wildly, picking up strength as the evening wore on.

"Whew!" Alexandre said, "I don't think you can get much closer to missing a storm than that! I sure am glad that we pushed ourselves tonight, or we would be guaranteed to have an uncomfortable morning tomorrow!"

"If you don't like it being that close, why don't you come up here sooner? If you were here two or three weeks ago, then you would have made it long before the storms."

"*Oui*, lad, but the king of France wants me to work much later than will allow that. The forts want us voyageurs to paddle as late into the season as possible, supplying them with winter provisions, which means that we aren't off until there is snow on the ground or ice in the rivers, whichever comes first. As you have well seen, once one storm comes, others are sure to follow, so the next clear break you get comes in the spring. *Non*, *monsieur*, it is necessary that we travel through the snow and storms to get to this cabin for the winter."

Francois nodded. He understood perfectly, as it made sense, but he didn't like the chances being taken to get here safely. It was all very risky, and Francois had never been one undaunted by risk. He had always preferred to live on the safe side, which was a good thing in its own way. But the frontier required risks, and the placid and hesitant frontiersman was often just waiting for his death.

Francois found his corner to be cozy and his blanket comfortable, but despite the roaring fire, there was still a chill in the night air. Francois shivered and wrapped the blanket more tightly around his body, but there wasn't much he could do. He had a hard time falling asleep that first night.

Over the next several days, Francois learned how to trap from his companions. He usually went with Alexandre, who showed him how to place the traps in the little channels in the ice that the beavers had made. By chopping a hole in the ice over the channel, the trap could be lowered into it and set, and then the beaver upon its next travel through that channel would be caught. Francois also learned how to set out traps for otters, minks, and foxes, as well as other animals that could be caught for their furs. After only a few days, Francois had taken a few traps out to set up his own trapline, but his traps were only set to catch land animals. The beaver furs were worth a lot of money in Paris, so the three more-experienced trappers focused on those. There was a big difference in price between a decent beaver fur and an excellent beaver fur, and this trapping crew wanted all of their beaver furs to be excellent.

Francois learned how to skin the furs from Eugene, and he learned how to stretch them from Pierre. He was a fast learner so it didn't take long for him to be doing the whole process on his own. He was eager to be an independent coureur de bois.

One day, as Francois was checking his traps, he heard a gunshot off to the west, followed by a wild scream. He was used to gunshots, as many of the trapped animals had to be shot when found, but the scream that had followed this gunshot was a suspicious occurrence as none of Francois's companions were bad shots. The sounds had come from the direction where Pierre's trapline was, so Francois immediately picked up his toboggan pull string and headed in that direction. As he ran through the snowy forest, he drew his tomahawk.

He reached Pierre's trapline to find Pierre skinning a lynx. Francois was about to commend Pierre on the catch when he noticed that the lynx hadn't been trapped.

"What happened?" Francois asked.

"This thief tried to steal the hare in my trap. I didn't like the idea," Pierre replied dryly with a slight hint of humor.

"So what screamed, the lynx or you?"

"The lynx," Pierre laughed, "it screamed at me just as I put the lead through its chest. It would have lunged at me, I think, if I hadn't shot it. It was hungry."

Francois nodded. He would have to be more careful when checking his traps from now on. The storms were keeping the prey inside, and the predators were often looking for easy meals to keep their stomachs full.

The bales of furs stacked in the shed outside grew in number almost daily. Francois was now bringing in his share of furs, and some of his otter and fox skins were as good as those of his companions. He was proud of his achievements, but he didn't let it get to him as he knew that the beaver pelts were the ones that would really make their winter efforts worthwhile, and he hadn't caught any of those yet.

One day in late January, Alexandre came out with a declaration that apparently Eugene and Pierre had heard before.

"I think it is time to go visiting," he said. Eugene and Pierre both nodded, but Francois couldn't hide his smile.

Who would they visit in this wilderness? The hibernating grizzly bears? Francois knew that Alexandre wouldn't be so foolish.

"We have been making good progress with our trapping, and I think that we can all take the day off from checking the lines. It is high time we went over to see Crooked Arrow and his tribe."

Francois nodded but couldn't hide his surprise. He hadn't realized that there were Indians living so close. As the men strapped on their snowshoes and headed off on their journey, Francois had to ask about the people they would see.

"Who are Crooked Arrow and his tribe?"

Eugene answered first. "They are Algonquin Indians, and they trap up in these woods much as we do. We visit them every year, for they are friends who can be trusted."

Francois had heard of the Algonquin Indians, but he didn't know much about them. Most of his knowledge of the native peoples was of the Haudenosaunees, as Francois had lived for a few weeks in one of their longhouses. He was eager to meet other tribes, however, and found this trip to be very exciting. The Algonquin tribes were friends with the French.

Crooked Arrow was a very old Indian. Francois was not sure that he should guess the man's age, but if he could have, he would have wondered if this Indian weren't ninety or ninety-five winters old. The man's face was wrinkled, but Francois recognized them as the wrinkles of experience and wisdom, and right away he knew that this old man was a respected person who had more than just survived the years—he had lived them.

The village the coureurs de bois found themselves in was relatively small but not unpopulated; there were many brown-skinned Indians wandering about, doing various chores. Francois noticed that all of them wore fur clothing, and he was amused as he mentally compared these people to the fashionable aristos in France who wore the same furs for style. On one continent, pelts meant fashion; on the other, warmth. In both, however, pelts meant money, which is why the fur trade was thriving.

Francois knew that the coureurs de bois didn't have any items to trade for the Indians' furs, but these Indians didn't seem to mind. They would have, but Alexandre had been coming up to these woods for many years now, and each winter he had come to trap, not trade. He wasn't the typical frontiersman who came through these woods, but he was a good friend, and a noble companion. The Algonquins whom he visited with each year had come to know him for who he was, so they did not mind the fact that he was not like the other coureurs de bois. He was one of their favorite Frenchmen, and Francois noticed the respect and admiration they gave him.

The midday meal was a sumptuous affair, and Francois ate until he was completely filled. He hadn't realized how much he had missed woman-cooked food because when you're a starving voyageur you don't complain much about what goes into your guts. He had never thought of voyageur food as all that distasteful, but it sure did blanch when compared to the venison he was eating now.

After the meal, Alexandre and Crooked Arrow began a long talk about New France and their friendship. Francois couldn't understand the chief's words, but occasionally, Eugene would help him, or Pierre. They had both learned some of the Algonquin language last year when they had trapped with Alexandre, so they knew some of what was being said, but they still weren't able to keep themselves or Francois informed of the whole discussion.

"He just complained that the French are showing friendship to the Iroquois Confederacy, especially the Seneca, when the Algonquin tribes have been more loyal to King Louis." Francois wouldn't have known what was said if Eugene hadn't translated; but the chief's expression told much of the message on its own.

Alexandre talked calmly, responding to Crooked Arrow's complaint, but Eugene couldn't understand what he said. Fortunately, Pierre did.

"He just said that the French wish to be the friends of all native peoples and that they only wish to trade for the furs that the Indians have trapped. They wish to show no favoritism to any tribes, but be impartial in every respect. Any fur-trading Indian is a friend of the French."

Francois knew that the Indians facing him may not like this speech, but he knew that it was true: France only wanted to trade for the furs of the natives, and any Indian with furs to trade would be King Louis's friend. Francois hoped that the Indians understood because they were sitting between the Frenchmen and the door to the lodge—escape would be impossible.

"Whew, that was the closest I've ever come to fighting them!" Alexandre sighed with relief as they trudged home the next day. "They were ready to fight if I said one wrong word."

Francois shivered at the thought of how close they had come to being killed. He didn't like the margin by which they had escaped. It was all way too close.

"Will we go back to see them again?" Francois asked.

"I don't believe so," Alexandre replied. "Normally I would return several times, but that meeting was too close for me. I think I'll keep my distance this winter."

Francois shivered again. If Alexandre was worried about how that meeting had gone, then something was wrong indeed. He hoped that they wouldn't go back. And then, when a terrible thought popped into his head, he dearly wished against that possibility too: he hoped that Crooked Arrow's people wouldn't come looking for them.

As the weeks dragged by, Francois found himself getting bored by the repetitive lifestyle he was living. Each day only meant another long hike through the woods, and

Francois often came home cold and weary after checking his trapline.

Then came a blow that no one had expected. Pierre had been out checking his beaver traps by the river and had seen that one of them held an animal. He walked over to the trap on the ice and lifted the trap from the water. Sure enough, a fine-skinned beaver was dead from the large steel jaws. Pierre took it out and reset the trap, but when he turned to go, his snowshoe fell through part of the beaver shaft and lodged there. Pierre knew that he was in a bad situation, but the snowshoe was jammed in a way that denied access to the straps that held his foot in it. As Pierre twisted and pulled to break free, the ice beneath him gave way, and he was dropped right into the icy river. The ice in that spot had been thinned by the beavers, but one couldn't tell that by looking through from the top. The under-ice current raged in fury, trying to drag Pierre beneath its icy blanket, but Pierre managed to hold on and stay afloat.

The current was swift, and its force and speed were draining Pierre's energy fast, but Pierre stubbornly held on for his life as his body temperature steadily fell. He knew that he didn't have much time, and he earnestly prayed that his companions would come looking for him soon. If they didn't, he knew that he would be dead before nightfall.

His teeth were chattering, his body shivering, but still he held on. He wasn't ready to give up yet.

15

FRANCOIS FOUND IT hard to believe that he had caught so many furs on the day's round. He hadn't had such a good catch in weeks, and he felt excitement over the creatures caught—most of them had very good pelts.

Alexandre arrived home next, toting four fine beaver skins among other pelts. Francois was humbled by this newest catch and found his conscience reprimanding himself for being so prideful.

Eugene arrived, and his day's round had been very poor. He had only a few bodies to skin, and several of them were not even great pelts. He finished his skinning and stretching first, so he was elected to make supper for the evening. He left to do so with a bit of a grudge: he had been the cook a fair amount over the past week.

As Francois and Alexandre finished caring for their skins, and the wafts of supper cooking began spewing forth from the chimney, Francois noticed with sudden shock that Pierre had not yet joined them.

"Alexandre, I just realized that Pierre has not arrived yet. I know that he has the largest trapline next to yours, but he shouldn't be this long in returning even if every trap was full."

"*Oui*, lad, I agree with you. I have been so focused on these pelts that I didn't even think about our friend. We'd best go out after him."

Francois nodded. "I will start out now," he said.

"Now hold on a minute, son," Alexandre interrupted. "I know Pierre probably better than anyone in this world. Like you said, he is most assuredly in trouble, or else he would be here. We have to prepare for the worst. Get your toboggan, and I will get some blankets from the cabin and tell Eugene that we will be out. I will also grab some herbs and such things, just in case he needs attention that can't wait till we get back here."

Francois shuddered at the idea. He seriously hoped that Pierre would not be *that* bad.

In a few minutes, they were ready; pointing their feet in the direction of Pierre's trapline, they started off.

"At least he got a ways before trouble hit him," Alexandre remarked dryly. "We're almost to the end, and there's no sign of him."

"Maybe he *was* just running behind. He could be back at the cabin by now."

"Indeed, he could be. But we're not taking that chance. If he is, we will meet him when we return. But we won't return until we have traveled the whole line, just in case."

Francois nodded. He agreed with Alexandre's plan. Then a horrible idea hit him.

"Alexandre! What if Pierre was captured by Indians!"

"Most unlikely, lad. The Indians up this way are all friendly with the French, and I wouldn't expect them to behave otherwise, even though they were a bit frightening back when we visited them. They are our friends, and as far as they are concerned, Pierre is safe."

They continued on in silence for many minutes. After a while, Alexandre broke it.

"He really waited to go down until the very end." He chuckled. "Plucky of him, for sure. But it is a good thing, really."

"Why is it good?" Francois asked, puzzled.

"Because it means that whatever happened, happened later in the day. So our chances of finding him alive are that much larger, and his chances of survival are that much larger as well. We shall see when we find him."

Francois nodded again, and they again traveled in silence for many minutes. Then an ugly thought flashed through Francois's head, and he had a bad feeling that he was right.

"Alexandre! *La riviere!*"

Alexandre's face went white.

"That's it, boy!" he shouted, and they both took off running as fast as their snowshoes would allow them to go, Francois still pulling the toboggan behind him.

When they reached the river, they both stood looking for only a few seconds. They saw it all: the trap hole, the beaver, the hole in the ice, and Pierre, barely conscious, gripping onto the edge of the ice. His face was white, and Francois wondered how he had managed to hold on for all this time.

They rushed down there, but their hurry was slowed down when they reached the river—they didn't want to join Pierre at his level. As they crept across the ice, they began calling to Pierre, telling him to hold on for just a few more minutes. He didn't respond.

When they reached him, Alexandre grabbed one of his arms, and Francois grabbed the other, and they began pulling him as hard as they could.

"I didn't think to bring a rope!" Alexandre cursed himself as they tugged at the limp body.

After several good pulls, Pierre was rescued from his precarious position, and Alexandre and Francois breathed sighs of relief. But their relief faded quickly as they noticed Pierre's state. He was now unconscious, and his face was almost as white as the snow and ice he was lying on. The men exchanged worried looks, and then Alexandre's experience took charge.

"Francois, bring the toboggan over as close to the river as you can get it. Make sure it is in a place that we can easily get it out of as well."

Francois moved to do as bidden, and when he had brought the toboggan close, he pushed the blankets off it.

"Do you want me to bring you your herbs?" Francois asked.

"Not much herbs will do. He's in a really bad way. The best thing we can do for him is get him to the cabin as soon as possible."

Francois's eyes gave away his shock and worry as he ran to help Alexandre lift the body into the sled. It was not an easy task, but they somehow managed to do it in reasonable time. Then packing the blankets around Pierre as tightly as they could, they headed off for the cabin at a dead run, both men pulling the toboggan together.

They continued to follow Pierre's trapline, as that route was now shorter than backtracking would have been. The night had come upon them, and they were now moving more by knowledge of the area than by sight.

They arrived about half an hour later and were met by an extremely worried Eugene, who had been considering coming out after them to help out. However, knowing that he would have been far behind them, he had made the hard decision to stay at the cabin and wait.

All three men hurriedly took Pierre inside to his bed, and each one gave up blankets for him. Eugene brought a cup of hot coffee and then slowly poured it down Pierre's throat.

Alexandre pulled Pierre's soaked pants off him and replaced them with his own second pair, while Francois continued to bank the chilled body with blankets. After the pants and blankets were in place, Alexandre began looking through all of his herbs and medicines, searching for anything that might help his friend's condition. He found none.

After the initial rush, the Frenchmen found themselves caught in a battle of time. Time was all that was left. They sat waiting, hoping for some sign of life, but as the hours dragged by, there was none.

All three men were exhausted and hungry, but no one slept or ate. Their eyelids were heavy, barely staying open, but they refused to capitulate to the urge they felt. Their friend was in a very bad way, and no man planned to be sleeping when signs of life or death occurred.

All through the night, they sat vigil with their friend. No one spoke, no one cried, no one even cleared his throat. Each one barely breathed as if their own breaths of life would rob their still friend of his. Such was the night that these devoted men endured. It was by far the longest of their lives.

Morning came, and with it, no relief. Pierre still was an unconscious form on his bed, wrapped in blankets and filled with coffee. The food that Eugene had prepared had burned to charred waste long before, but the coffee pot was empty due to Pierre's frequent sips. He was the only person who had received nourishment since the afternoon before.

Eugene was dispatched to go give word to Crooked Arrow's tribe to see if they had any herbs or medicines that would help Pierre recover from his hypothermia. Crooked Arrow himself came to visit, bringing with him several women and medicine men, but none of their remedies worked. It seemed that Pierre had no hope of recovery.

Occasionally, Pierre would cry out in his delirium, calling out words and sentences that didn't make sense. Often, his words were not even understandable, and his blue fingers and still-shivering body were proof that he had been hit hard. Alexandre knew that he had been in the river way too long, and that his recovery was very unlikely.

The traplines needed to be checked, and the men needed food and rest, but none of these necessities occurred. The men were too worried about their friend to think of anything else. He was slowly deteriorating, and well they knew it. Depressing as the fact was to them, they couldn't keep it out because they knew that it was true—Pierre was dying.

It happened the next afternoon. Alexandre had just brought in some more wood for the fire, Eugene had coffee brewing, and Francois was sitting in his bed corner, staring at the opposite wall. Pierre's voice pierced the dull stillness, and three heads turned to him as one. His body shivered and shook in wild, uncoordinated movements, and his blue left hand feebly raised up into the air a few inches. He called out a few more words that his companions could not understand, and then he said, very softly, "I have paddled this river and have now reached the ocean."

His hand fell slowly back to the ground and lay still, and his last breath was so labored that it echoed within the log walls. The silence was so thick that one could have heard a moccasined footstep on a fur blanket, and the men stood in their transfixion for many minutes, the realization of what had just occurred slowly inhabiting their brains.

Pierre was dead.

16

It took a long time for Francois and his companions to realize it. It took even longer for them to get used to it. But they never got over it. Pierre was often a grumpy, bossy companion, but he was still a companion, and he never deserted someone traveling with him. He was a man to ride the rivers with if ever a man was, and his three surviving companions realized it full well.

When spring finally came, the three coureurs de bois baled their furs and began taking trips to the place where they had left their canoes in the fall. When their canoes were loaded, they propped their toboggans up against the side of the shed and left the snug cabin for another summer. The soldiers in New France were hungry, and these men were needed to paddle canoes and bateaux filled with food for all the western forts.

It took a day or two for Francois to get used to paddling again, as he had not done so for several months. Once he did get his rhythm back, however, he was able to keep pace just as well as Alexandre or Eugene. Since Pierre was no longer with them, Alexandre paddled one canoe by himself while Francois and Eugene shared the other one. To make up for the extra burden on Alexandre, they had loaded his canoe with their belongings and food while Francois and Eugene carried most of the heavy fur bales. It didn't make much difference overall, but it still helped some.

"Ah, Montreal! 'Tis been a fair piece since I saw you, *oui*!" Alexandre called out as the city came into view. The three Frenchmen had paddled their canoes into the Saint Lawrence River the day before, just south of Montreal, and now were within sight of its grand buildings.

"Oh, but it does seem such a long time since we last laid eyes upon this island!" Francois shouted above the noise of the river. "She is still as beautiful as she was last fall."

"*Oui*, that she is!" Eugene replied to his companions. "A grand sight to the eyes of a Frenchman! May the flag of France fly long over her walls!"

At these words, the spirits of the voyageurs fell. All three men wished for their flag to fly over Montreal, but all knew the dim hopes facing New France. The losses of forts Duquesne and Louisburg last year, combined with the destruction of Fort Frontenac, seriously depleted the nation's resources and strategic locations. Outnumbered and outgunned, the French were beginning to feel some pressure from the invading British armies.

The price of the furs, though lower than ideal, was still enough to supply Alexandre's crew with the year's necessities. After the items had been bartered for and then loaded onto the two canoes, Alexandre began looking to fill his ranks with voyageurs for the year's first trip. Fifty canoes loaded with flour, cornmeal, salt, and gunpowder were waiting to be taken to Fort Niagara, and Alexandre had been charged with the task of overseeing their safe delivery. At once, he began his process of selection. Walking through the city's streets, he chose many of the poorer men to join him. Many who had done voyageuring for Alexandre in the past showed up again, and all who had shown themselves to be hard workers were given jobs. Alexandre then appointed one man in each canoe to be in charge of that canoe's activity, including paddling, cooking, sleeping, loading, and unloading. Only men who had worked for Alexandre previously were given these jobs, and Francois and Eugene were both among the men given a canoe to oversee. Francois could not help but feel pride at the promotion as it showed him how much he was appreciated by Alexandre and how well he must really be doing in New France. All at once, his father's quote came back to him: "Work hard, my son. Never give anyone a reason to call you lazy." He thought about his family back in France and wished that he could let them know how he fared.

À Saint-Malo beau port de mer,
À Saint-Malo beau port de mer,
Trois gro navires sont arrivés.

Nous irons sur l'eau,
Nous y prom-promener
Nous iron jouier dans l'île.

Chargés d'avoin, chargés de blé
Chargés d'avoin, chargés de blé
Trois dames s'en vont les marchander.

Nous irons sur l'eau,
Nous y prom-promener
Nous iron jouier dans l'île.

"Pull your weight, Bastogne!" Francois yelled to the voyageur slacking off in the back of the canoe. "Let me see you work!"

Grudgingly, the buckskin-clad ruffian began paddling again with the rest of the crew.

"Why are some of us not allowed to take breaks?" he asked mischievously. "There are more than enough men on this boat to allow some to rest."

"Do not make me mad, Bastogne," Francois warned with slightly lowered head and eyebrows, "and do not make me take this to Alexandre."

The voyageur stopped protesting, but his scowl and body language told Francois that he was far from satisfied with how the conversation had ended. Sighing, Francois turned back around on his bench to face forward and dipped his paddle into the Saint Lawrence. Bastogne had been the only troublemaker since their departure two days ago, but he had more than made up for the rest of the crew's respect. His nature was to disagree with whoever was in authority over him, and he did it very well. He had managed to argue with his superiors about almost every decision they had made since they left Montreal, and his status had no chance of improving because of it. His position for this trip was likely to remain at the bottom—a paddler just along for the ride.

Sighing again, Francois took another long stroke with his paddle.

"There she is! The ruins of Fort Frontenac! We have reached Lake Ontario once more!"

Francois looked up at Alexandre's shouting.

"The supplies that we lost last year were very costly," one of Francois's boatmen whispered quietly, "plus the loss of the boats the English took. Thank God that they left it shortly afterward or we would no longer be able to supply Fort Niagara and the other forts to the west."

Francois only nodded, thinking about what the voyageur had said. It was true that the loss of supplies to the English had been very costly, and they could ill afford to lose the ships as well. But the ground was the most strategic part of Frontenac, and that was still in French control. Supplies can be replaced and boats rebuilt much easier than land retaken, and the thought gave Francois courage as he paddled his way into the lake.

"I hope that the king sends over more soldiers to garrison these forts," one of the bearded gruff paddlers grumbled, "because if he does not, then soon there may not be any forts left to garrison. Duquesne is lost, Louisburg is lost, the English are amassing an army to attack Quebec, and Fort Niagara will be attacked soon as well."

"Are they building an army to take Niagara?" Francois asked, surprised at the news.

"Not especially as far as I have heard," the voyageur corrected, "but why not? If Niagara falls, then all of the western forts fall as well. Quebec does not stand much of a chance unless Montcalm stays nestled in the heights. Still, sooner or later, Montreal and Niagara will be under fire from English artillery."

Francois sobered at the thought. He could not imagine Fort Niagara being taken by the English. Or Montreal for that matter. They were all part of his experience in New France, and he just could not picture life without them. And then, suddenly, Francois began wondering what he would do if New France were taken over completely, and the French people exiled or imprisoned. This was the best life that Francois could ever dare hope to live, and yet, as he thought about the nation's situation, he realized how dire it was. If Quebec fell, then much was lost, and most hope was gone. If Niagara fell, then the French would be all but finished. The last blow would be Montreal. But if both Quebec and Niagara fell, then Montreal's doom would be certain. Francois didn't much like the idea.

Then, slowly, one of the voyageurs in one of the other canoes began to sing. Unlike most of the songs that these men sang, however, this song was sad and slow. Soon others had joined in until over half of the flotilla's paddlers were singing along. Francois sang as best he could, but he found it hard to sing when his heart weighed so heavily in his chest, hindering his breathing. His heart was so heavy that he suddenly felt very weak and drained, and he found it hard to paddle his share of the boat's weight. Determined to do his share, Francois took a deep breath and forced himself to carry on with the task at hand. Sentiments and worries could wait until later.

"Load up! Paddle away! Quick!" Alexandre yelled to his workers as they finished their breakfast.

Francois looked up, startled at Alexandre's command. A bullet just missed his head.

Guns went off in the woods, and then there came the sound of Indian war yells. Grabbing his gear, Francois joined the rest of the crew running to the canoes to load up.

"You, you, and you," Alexandre yelled above the gunshots and war cries, "pick up your muskets and return fire. The rest of us will join you when we have finished loading the boats."

Soon the Frenchmen were sounding gunshots of their own. The Indians kept up the attack for a few more minutes, then withdrew as quickly and silently as they had appeared. Sighing deeply and wiping his forehead, Alexandre voiced his fears.

"That, my fellows, signals the beginning of the end of New France."

Puzzled, Francois could only ask, "Why?"

"Because, lad, those were Canadian Mohawk Indians who just attacked us."

"But they are our allies!" Francois was incredulous.

"*Were* our allies," Alexandre corrected. "Something must have changed."

"Does that mean that we are constantly in danger from attack?" one of the younger, newer voyageurs asked.

"We are always in danger," Alexandre explained, "but now even more than ever."

"Do you think that the Canadian Mohawks will attack again soon?" Francois asked.

"I do not believe so. I got a good look at the group that just attacked us, and it was comprised of only a few young warriors. Itching for scalps, I should think. But it does not bode well. They are still Canadian Mohawks, and they would not have attacked us unless the whole Canadian Mohawk nation was joining the English. We must be more alert than ever if we want to reach Fort Niagara safely."

Nodding, Francois turned and climbed into his canoe. The last few voyageurs on shore climbed into their various canoes, and then the flotilla was off once again headed for the Niagara Peninsula.

17

Francois saw the flag first. The day had started out rainy with thick fog hanging over the lake but had gradually cleared after the sun had risen. As it had, visibility had improved to the point where Francois could now see the south shore of the lake. Knowing that the fort was close to view, he had been watching the horizon with peeled eyes, hoping to be the first to glimpse it fluttering in the Niagara breeze.

"There it is! The flag of France still flies!" Francois shouted for all of the crew to hear.

Heads turned, paddles stopped momentarily, and all 405 voyageurs felt their hearts flutter as they experienced the inspiration of watching their nation's flag fly proudly over the stone ramparts of the fort. Each man felt a new surge of devotion wash through him, each took on a new burden of responsibility, and each one dug into his paddle a little more in the hope of arriving at the fort sooner.

"That is a relief to see that she is still French," one of the pessimistic boatmen mumbled for all in the canoe to hear. "I was afraid that the English would have come and taken her over the winter. It wouldn't have taken much."

"I respectfully disagree," Francois objected. "Fort Niagara is by no means impenetrable or invincible, but she is strong, and the walls are solid. No secret military expedition carried out in the dead of winter could take her. Not in the weather of New France. She would not be such an easy capture, I can assure you."

The voyageur only scowled at that, then muttered, "I think that a few Indians could have done it if they were of a mind to. One fort sitting in the middle of a forest is not very defensible, no matter how solid its walls are."

"First of all, Indians could *not* take Fort Niagara. They do not have the artillery or military genius that the capture of such a fort requires. And besides, even if Fort Niagara had indeed been taken, we would have heard about it long before now."

The voyageur gave Francois a withering look of contempt, but he shut his mouth.

Sighing deeply, Francois turned to the rest of his crew.

"The fort needs these supplies," he announced, though it was not news. "They have been cut off from civilization for nearly five months, and we have no way of knowing what their storehouse looks like. It may still have provisions remaining, or it may have run out three weeks ago. Our job is to get these goods to them as soon as we possibly can to ensure that the fort's inhabitants are fed as they should be—as soldiers and citizens of France!"

A cheer went up from Francois's canoe, and his men put extra weight into their paddles for the rest of the afternoon. In no time at all, they were at the head of the flotilla and, as a result, were the first boat to beach and unload when the evening came.

"If we make good time tomorrow, then we may reach the fort by midafternoon," Alexandre told his assembled crew. "If, however, we do not make good time tomorrow, then we should arrive by midmorning of the second day. Get plenty of rest this evening, gentlemen, for we shall push very hard to arrive tomorrow afternoon."

Every man nodded solemnly and lay down to get some sleep.

The following day was gorgeous, and the voyageurs had no trouble reaching Fort Niagara that afternoon. As they neared the small dock by the lower village, Francois began to think of all his friends at the fort and wondered how they had fared throughout the winter.

I cannot wait to see Alphonse's face when we show him all this flour! Francois thought to himself as the boat hit the shore.

He didn't have long to wait. Alphonse was among the group of Frenchmen and Indians waiting at the dock for the flotilla to land. Francois immediately sought out his friend and did get to see the baker's expression as the flour was unloaded. It made the trip more than worth it for the voyageur.

Bertrand arrived shortly after the boats landed, and the parade began. The canoes were relieved of their precious bundles, and those bundles were carried up the hill to the fort's storehouse where Alphonse would retrieve them when his supply in the bakehouse ran low.

It took about one hour for all the canoes to be unloaded, and then the conversations began. And the tours, for many of this year's crew had never been to Fort Niagara before for one reason or another. As the guests were shown the fort's buildings and ramparts and walked through the fort's spacious parade ground, they were impressed by the genius behind the fort's structure and location. Even Richard, the boatman from Francois's canoe who was surprised that the fort had survived the winter, had to admit that the fort would be a very difficult capture. The only thing lacking, he thought to himself, is sufficient numbers of soldiers to garrison it.

Francois was glad to be back with his friends at the fort, but he noticed a different attitude among them now that had not been present when he had left in the fall. Many of the inhabitants worked with less fervor and joy than they used to, and Francois knew that something was wrong. Wanting to know the reason, he sought out a time to speak with one of his friends about it. And his first chance came when he and Bertrand were taking a walk outside the fort.

"Bertrand, why is everyone inside the fort so quiet and somber? The atmosphere is not nearly as joyful as it was last fall."

Bertrand sighed deeply, for he knew the answer only too well. He had, after all, been fighting the same depression for close to two weeks.

"There are rumors going around that the English are assembling an army near Albany to come and take this fort."

"You mean attack it," Francois corrected.

"*Non*, I mean *take* it," Bertrand replied with just a hint of bitterness. "This fort is strong, *oui*, but she is not properly garrisoned, and the English have blockaded the coast. No more ships will come, Francois. No more soldiers from home to increase our numbers. General Montcalm has more troops up at Quebec, but he is also expecting an attack and will not send us any of his army. Every other large army to speak of is garrisoned either at Montreal or one of the other forts in the territory. *Non*, Francois, help will not come to us."

"What about the Indians?" Francois asked with a hint of pride.

Why had Bertrand not thought of that?

"What Indians?" Bertrand replied nastily. "Our only Indian allies lie to the west of here, in the Ohio Valley and farther westward. They will not come this far just to help us fight the English. We have to be able to stand up for ourselves."

"But who says that we have to get help from that far away? Why can't the Senecas help us?"

"The Senecas are leaving us, Francois," Bertrand replied quietly.

"What?" Francois gasped.

"*Oui*, it is indeed true. Many have already left, others have threatened to, most will not change their minds. We have fought long and hard for an alliance with the Iroquois Confederacy, and now it appears that the English will defeat us. That is a far greater blow than the losses of Louisburg, Duquesne, and Frontenac combined!"

Neither one spoke for the rest of the walk, though each one heard many voices in his own mind. Both thought of the fort's chances of survival, and neither one liked the odds.

A few days later after most of the voyageurs had already left to return to Montreal, Francois was met in the woods by a band of painted Indian warriors. Each one looked fierce, but not one was holding a weapon in his hands. Wishing for control of his pumping heart, Francois offered to take them to Captain Pouchot, the new commander of the fort. Their leader, who spoke some French, was able to tell Francois that was their reason for coming. Nodding quickly, Francois turned to the fort, not much liking the fact that he could not see the vicious humans walking behind him. As they neared the gate of the Six Nations, Francois could see the guards on duty watching him to see if he brought these Indians willingly. Francois made signs to assure them that the Indians came in peace and sent a nearby off-duty soldier to summon the commandant and his staff.

It was only a few minutes before Captain Pouchot and his officers sat facing this group of Seneca Indians in one of the castle's large rooms. There was some general conversation, mostly the commandant asking how the tribe's women and children fared, before the two groups discussed the business at hand. Captain Pouchot started it. "I would like to invite our Seneca brothers to share with us what has brought them here as the journey you have taken shows that something troubles you greatly. This journey is hard and long. Only men would dare to take it, and only men would reach their destination safely. The fact that you warriors are standing here before me proves that you are men."

The Senecas were pleased with this speech, and the commandant could feel their attitudes changing. They had come with problems, but his flattery had softened their hearts and words. It was a few moments before the leader spoke, and when he did, his words were much calmer than any of the French officers had expected them to be.

"The Beaver tribe of the Seneca nation would like to thank the French for welcoming us to their fort. The French speak truth. It is a long and difficult journey for the warriors to make, but it is worth the effort seeing the French when we arrive. We thank the French for their concern for our women and children and are pleased to inform them that our tribe was left in good health."

Captain Pouchot bowed gracefully and acknowledged the happiness of his nation for the Senecas' well-being. However, he noticed something in the leader's manner that worried him besides the fact that the leader's speech had not included the word *friend*.

"I would like to invite our brothers the Senecas to share their troubles, fears, and thoughts with their friends, the French," the commandant continued. "And may the great King Louis be able to grant the Senecas their desires."

At this, the leader's eyes turned cold. "The French are no longer our brothers, for they do not show the care that true brothers must show. They do not give us enough flour and cornmeal to feed our families, and they do not protect us from our enemies, the Mohawks. The Mohawks get many beautiful gifts while we must trade furs for our gifts. These are not gifts. Many Senecas have left to join the English, and they also receive many gifts."

"We thank our brothers the Senecas for their openness in this matter. Many of the Senecas have left to join the English without first asking us for their gifts. For your loyalty to King Louis, we shall give you many presents to take back to your village. Lieutenant, see to it."

The dispatched officer left immediately to collect some items from the trade room. When he returned, the Indians' eyes lit up, but the leader was firm.

"These gifts no good. The English give beads and red cloth, not knives and kettles. We have enough kettles, we have enough knives. Give us beads and red cloth so our women will be as lovely as the Mohawk women."

The commandant cringed inwardly. How could he explain that there was no more red cloth in the trade room? And that the beads were low? The Indians would not understand, but he must provide these items for them. The survival of New France depended on it.

"I shall give you the beads you ask for, but the red cloth shall have to be ordered from one of our cities. I will give you the knives and kettles along with the beads, as well as powder and shot for your muskets. May the sun forever shine on our Seneca brothers, and may the spirits grant them safe travel back to their village!"

The leader's eyes turned ugly. "This is the last time that we come to visit the French," he said, hatred permeating from his very being. "The English give red cloth in abundance when their allies ask, but the French tell their allies to wait. We have waited long enough. Let the spirits decide the fate of the French. We shall go to the English."

The commandant's face was solemn as the warriors filed out, and the lines on his forehead showed his worry and age. The past few weeks had been very hard on him, and this was becoming more than he could take. One more village of Seneca Indians had left to join the English, which both decreased his numbers and increased the enemy's. Once the Indians were gone, the commandant shook his head sadly. These defections needed to be stopped, but there was nothing he could do.

Francois had waited in the castle's main room while the meeting had taken place, and now he watched from his position near the well as the Indians left the building.

"*Adieu*, Francois."

Francois looked up, startled. Who had spoken to him? He looked around the room before realizing that one of the Indians was looking back at him. Francois gazed at the Indian's face before he stepped out of the door and then was left to puzzle at the strange occurrence. Had he seen that Indian before? Francois didn't think so, yet at the same time, something about the Indian did seem familiar. As Francois tried to picture the Indian's face in his past, he suddenly saw in his mind a vivid picture of a band of Indians standing before him, faces painted. Scalps hung at their belts suspended next to tomahawks and knives. And then, realization flooded his mind as he watched one of the warriors lift his bow.

That was it! That warrior from the group that Francois had journeyed with last summer had just walked out of the French castle! Excitement surged through Francois as he thought of the friendships that could be rekindled because of the meeting, and then it all died quickly as he remembered that the group had left to join the English. Disturbed, Francois asked around to see if the whole village was joining the English or just the one group of warriors. At the message from one of the other soldiers who had heard it from an officer, Francois felt his heart sink low. All of his friends, all of the days and nights spent with them, had been for nothing. They had played together, fought together, traveled together as comrades, and now they were parting to go their separate ways. Now they were enemies.

"'Tis indeed a shame, lad," Alexandre told Francois that night after he had been informed of the day's events, "and I am very sorry that you have to experience the loss of friends like that."

"We are no longer friends," Francois replied sadly.

"I would not be so quick to sever ties, Francois," Alexandre warned. "We do not know for sure that the whole village is leaving us, and if you allow your heart to harden, then it will be much harder to soften it later."

"What is the point? How do we know that some in the village have stayed on our side?"

"That is exactly my point," Alexandre said, "we have no way of knowing. That is why we must wait before we make up our minds to be friendly or unfriendly. If some of those Indians are still on our side, then you becoming an enemy will sever what is still a lasting friendship."

Francois nodded. It made sense to him, but he found it hard to believe that the rest of the tribe had stayed with the French. They had struck him as being a very close-knit group, and they had given Francois the impression that they would not split up based on opinions. He was not even sure if it was possible for them to *have* different opinions.

"I just wish that I had not gone and made friends with them in the first place, then this would not be so hard," Francois lamented after a few minutes' silence.

"I know how you feel, son," Alexandre encouraged back.

"You do?"

"*Oui.* I once had a really good Indian friend. His name was Canaraucas. He was an Oneida, back when the Oneidas were more open to us French. Canaraucas and I went on several hunts together, and once we canoed all the way to Fort Detroit. I thought that our friendship would last forever, but the day came when the Oneidas had to make a final decision: us or the English. They chose the English, and Canaraucas went with them. I thought that he was deserting me, that he was a traitor, but I know better now. He had a duty to his tribe, and his tribe had joined the English. Though he fights with the English now, he is still my friend. I will love him as a brother forever."

"But what if he tried to kill you? Wouldn't you think that he does not want to be your friend and is therefore your enemy?"

"I have thought long and hard about that. It is not a restful thought, let me assure you. But I can say with confidence that he would still be my brother at heart, for I cannot begrudge any man who does his duty. And if Canaraucas were to face me in battle or elsewhere, it would be his duty to kill me. Or die trying. I do not believe that I could kill him, but he is an Indian. He is a warrior. He would find it much easier to do his duty than I mine. If he killed me, then *non*, I would not hold it against him. After all, did not Jesus Christ do the same thing for those soldiers who killed Him? I must seek to follow His example, Francois. That is the ultimate measure of a man."

Francois had forgotten how good a speaker Alexandre was. Watching him now, he saw him once again as a man to stand by, a man to die for. Alexandre was a man to walk the trails with, and Francois was proud to be able to say that he had walked many trails and paddled many canoes with the man sitting across the campfire from him. Many of Francois's countrymen would have given anything to sit beside King Louis XV, or General Montcalm, or Governor-General Vaudreuil-Cavagnial, and well he knew it. But he would rather sit beside Alexandre than any of these men as Alexandre possessed a kind of nobility that each of these men lacked, and he had a humble, hardworking character that all of these men could only wish they had. No, Alexandre was the better companion for Francois and the better teacher. Francois owed everything he had, everything he knew about survival, even his own life, to this man; and he was more grateful than words could ever say.

18

I<small>T WAS A</small> rainy day to hunt, but the remaining voyageurs needed meat. Since many of them were busy repairing their canoes and preparing animal pelts, Francois volunteered to go get some food. Grabbing his musket and shot bag, he started off through the woods to the southeast.

After a few minutes, he met up with a group of voyageurs leaving on a raid. They were heading down to the Pennsylvania frontier, where they would attack a few of the lonely outposts and cause some mischief. Since these men had come to Fort Niagara with Alexandre, Francois knew them all.

"Are you going straight to the English settlements?" he asked, unsure of their intentions.

"*Non*, we will head southwest to the Ohio River Valley where we will meet up with some scalp-seeking warriors.

With increased numbers, we will be able to do more damage. From there we will head straight into English territory."

"What tribe will your Indian allies be from? Shawnee?"

"*Non*, the Shawnee made a treaty with the English last year, so they are no longer safe to travel with. Instead, we will probably seek out a group of Ottawa warriors. They are still on our side and will be happy to join us on our raid, I am sure."

Nodding, Francois bade them safe journey. *So the Shawnees have joined the English as well,* he thought to himself, shaking his head, *will it never end?* His thoughts were interrupted by the snap of a twig in the thicket to his left. Glancing around quickly, Francois saw nothing, so he dove to the ground and crawled under some nearby honeysuckle bushes for cover. As he tried to slow his heavy breathing, Francois slowly took in his surroundings. He was in a well-protected area with plenty of brush cover to screen his movements, so for the moment he was safe.

Whatever had made the twig snap had stopped moving as well, and Francois knew by the sound of the twig that the creature who had stepped on it was human: a deer would not have made such a loud snap. That being true, it was extremely unlikely that an Indian would have been that careless. That left two likely options: the creature currently sharing the woods with Francois was either French or English, and Francois did not like the chances that it was the latter.

There was a rustle of leaves off to Francois's left, and it was closer than the twig snap had been. Keeping his eyes open and focused on the forest around him, Francois blindly reached down to his belt and drew his tomahawk. Amid all of the brush, it would be harder for him to use his musket, especially if he had to resort to fighting hand-to-hand, and his bow and arrows would be equally useless in such a situation. That left only one option. Gripping his tomahawk in one hand and his just-drawn knife in the other, he was ready to take on the person nearby.

Lifting himself into a squatting position, Francois prepared to dash out into the open by the trail. Choosing where he would drop in the thickets across the way, he took one last look around. Movement about ten feet in front of him changed his plans for action, and he was forced to think quickly about his situation. The Indian before him raised his knife to throw but stopped suddenly and lowered it.

"Francois!"

It was the warrior who had left the castle the other evening with his band. He had returned.

At Francois's hesitation, the warrior laughed.

"Do not fear, brother, I am still on the side of the French."

"But…but, you left with the group…for Albany," Francois stumbled, trying to clear up the confusion in his mind.

"I could not stand with the French when my leader and my band stood against them, but I can still disagree with what they said."

"So does that mean that you—"

"I left them two suns ago to return here. I am ready to fight with my brothers the French. You are the first one I found."

"Why don't you return to your tribe?" Francois asked, not expecting the answer that was forthcoming.

"They have all left to join the English. Only a few wanted to stay, and those were taken care of in various ways. If you were to visit the village now, you would be tortured and killed as an enemy."

Francois felt like crying at the news. The whole tribe, his former friends, had turned away from their allegiance with the French to join the enemy. Francois had not a clue what could drive them to do it, but something obviously had. The minds of men change quickly, and what suits a man—especially an Indian—one day may not suit him so well the next. The French had suited the Seneca nation in days gone by, but a new day had dawned. The French were no longer satisfactory.

Turning to the warrior before him, Francois bade him welcome to fight alongside the French. Accepting the offer, the warrior followed him through the woods to the large stone walls of the fort. Francois decided to hunt for meat later; he had something to discuss with Captain Pouchot.

The warrior, whose name Francois discovered to be Silver Fox, was made welcome within the walls of the fort, though rather suspiciously at first. The commandant wanted to be sure that he was not a spy, but Francois assured him that Silver Fox meant no such harm, and he was given a chance. The commandant made him a hunter for the fort's food supply as well as a woodcutter. When the needs arose, he was to guide relations with other Indians in the region, especially the fast-defecting Seneca nation. Pleased with his new tasks, Silver Fox proved to be a good and loyal worker.

As time went on, Francois and Silver Fox spent increasingly more time hunting together in the forest. Francois was usually the one who brought in meat for the voyageur camp, and Silver Fox was constantly being dispatched by the Indians in the lower village or Alphonse to bring in meat to supplement their bread and vegetables.

On this particular day, Francois and Silver Fox were both hunting with bows in the woods directly east of the fort. They had traveled between two and three miles and so far had caught one rabbit and a brace of turkeys. As they surveyed the brush and clearings around them for signs of game, Francois broke their silence with a question that had been nagging him for a long time.

"Silver Fox, did Running Deer join the English?"

The Indian was silent for some time before responding. "*Oui*, he did."

"But did he want to, or did he do it just because the rest of the tribe did?"

"Do you really want me to tell you the truth, Francois?" Something in Silver Fox's tone warned Francois of what could be coming.

"*Oui*, I do, Silver Fox, even if it hurts to hear or comprehend."

"Most of the tribe wanted to join the English, yes, but our chief and several of the senior women did not. The discussions were often vicious between the two parties, and many hurtful things were said."

"I thought that you Indians respected your chiefs and women much more than we Europeans do," Francois remarked, confused by his friend's statement.

"There are renegades in every culture, Francois," Silver Fox said quietly, "and there are outcasts in every one as well."

"What is that supposed to mean?" Francois asked, fear and worry beginning to grow in his chest.

"The discussions became so fierce that they became arguments, and in one of them, the chief openly ridiculed one of the warriors. He called him a young and inexperienced scalp-seeker who needed to learn his place."

"Was it true?"

"*Oui*, it was, but the warrior would not hear of it. Instead, he killed the chief and left to join the English."

"But surely, it was not—"

"*Non*, it was not Running Deer who killed him. It was Running Deer's father. Running Deer had wanted to join the English anyway, but his life was in danger once his father had murdered the chief. He left before anyone could harm him, but his absence did not settle down those who remained. The whole village is in an uproar, Francois, and now that the chief is gone, the whole village is joining the English. There are not enough French-minded warriors left among them to prevent it. That is why I am here. I am a renegade, but they are all renegades as well. I have left the Senecas because they have left the French. There is no other way to stand up for what is right than to leave the party that is going astray."

Francois nodded, for that was all that he felt he could do. He felt very sorry for Running Deer, but most of his grief was in the fact that Running Deer had planned to join the English anyway. After all that Francois and Running Deer had done together in those few days at the Indian village, Francois now found it very hard to picture himself and the Indian as enemies. But this was war, and war has always been very good at making enemies. This Francois knew full well, though it ultimately did nothing to ease his sadness or answer his questions.

Then, suddenly, a buck jumped out of a thicket to Francois's left, and before it could jump back into the brush, it had absorbed one of the arrows from Francois's quiver. Stumbling to the ground, it lay its head on the dense carpet of leaves and ferns and knew no more.

19

"Do you really have to go, Alexandre?" Francois asked sadly. Alexandre and Silver Fox had been asked by Captain Pouchot to go on a special mission to Albany. Their task was to find out as much information as they could about the English army being assembled to attack Fort Niagara.

"*Oui*, lad, the commandant has asked me to go, and I cannot refuse him. Silver Fox and I will find out everything that the commandant needs to know and then return. You can wait here for us, and then we will return to Montreal together, or you can leave now, if you wish, and we will meet you there. Either way, Francois, I will return so that we can continue to paddle together. Don't you worry about that."

Francois smiled. If there was anything he was worried about, it was not that Alexandre would be killed on his upcoming expedition. It was just—*Hmmm*, thought

Francois, what is bothering me about this? I know that Alexandre will come back, but will he? What is this nagging feeling inside of me?

Try as he might, Francois could not put his finger on the source of his distress.

The morning was clear and lovely with a cool breeze blowing when Alexandre and Silver Fox shouldered their haversacks and shot bags and exited the fort through the gate of the Six Nations. Francois watched them from the parade ground until they entered the large stone building that housed the gates, and then he climbed the stairs to the earth and stone ramparts to watch them disappear into the forest. Francois felt a sense of inspiration as he watched them go, but the nagging feeling in his chest refused to leave him. Shrugging at its mystery, Francois descended to the parade ground level and began his daily tasks. His buckskin pants had a tear that needed to be patched, and his musket badly needed polishing. After these were completed, Francois ventured outside the fort to find a stone, which he then used to sharpen his knife and tomahawk. When those tasks were done, Francois headed to the bakehouse to chat with Alphonse while the baker waited for the day's bread to rise.

Alphonse was only too glad to have someone to talk to.

"How are things going, Francois?" he asked seriously after some general small talk.

"To be honest, not too well," Francois replied, and at Alphonse's prodding, he continued on with his feelings.

He told of his depression regarding the situation in New France, his sadness over the loss of his Seneca friends, and of his worry about Alexandre and Silver Fox.

"Well," Alphonse began after Francois had finished, "I can definitely appreciate the fact that you have several issues on your mind, and that alone is contributing much to your anxiety, I am sure. The rest of it, I believe, is because everything you are worried about involves close friends. But some of these issues are not worth worrying about. You have no control over the situation in New France. You are just one of the king's boatmen, Francois, not a general or the governor-general who ultimately makes the final decisions. As far as the matters with the Indians go, it is very hard to lose friends, especially close friends. But again, this matter is out of your hands as well. You cannot satisfy the Senecas on your own, and trying will only make you more depressed. King Louis cannot afford the gifts that the king of England can even if it were possible to ship them here. Now that the English control Louisburg and the coast, there is no hope of any help arriving from the mainland. Oh, to see our dear France again! I fear that there is no hope of that left for any of us. But we shall see. I may be wrong yet. After all, it is all in God's hands, and nothing is impossible with Him."

Francois nodded, but his demeanor and mood had not changed.

"And then there is Alexandre and Silver Fox. Do not worry about them, Francois. That is only a foolish waste of your time. Alexandre will return, no doubt. He is too wily and savvy for the English to catch him."

"But he is still human, Alphonse," Francois excused. "What if he runs into a group of Mohawk Indians, and they notice him before he notices them? They will not wait for him to be ready to fight."

"What you say is true indeed, Francois," Alphonse admitted, "but I sure would like to see the Indian who comes upon Alexandre unnoticed! Such a human would surely have to be a ghost if it were to be accomplished. No, Francois, people do not creep up on Alexandre. He waits for them to come too close, faking ignorance. Trust me, I have seen it before. Then when their confidence and cockiness is up, he kills them faster than you can blink your eye."

Francois blinked in amazement at Alphonse's words.

"You have seen him do this?" he asked, incredulous.

"I sure have," Alphonse replied, chuckling. "He did it against an Indian who wanted to catch a scalp from as close to Fort Niagara as he could get. He came too close. I heard the shuffle and tomahawk strike and turned to see Alexandre collecting the Indian's powder and shot. I had not even seen the Indian, but Alexandre told me that he had seen it when it had been over one hundred feet away. It had not pulled out its bow for one reason or another, so Alexandre let it approach. It has never ceased to amaze me how quickly he killed that Indian!"

Francois could not help but laugh along with Alphonse. It felt good. As he and Alphonse chuckled and shared a few more stories with each other, Francois realized how little he had laughed lately and how much it had affected him. Letting out some kind of emotion made him feel much better, and by the time he left the bakehouse just before high noon, his anxiety was low, and depression almost completely gone. Since his stomach was complaining of emptiness, Francois decided to head to the voyageur camp outside of the fort to get some dinner.

"Francois, Captain Pouchot would like to speak with you," Bertrand told his friend later that evening.

"Really? Why?" Francois asked, confused at the idea.

"I do not know the details," his friend replied, "but I have been told that it is important. You must come with me."

Francois obeyed, but the confusion still remained, fogging his mind. Why did the commandant want to speak with him? Was there news? Trouble? Had he heard from Alexandre? Francois's heart leaped within his chest at the idea. Such a circumstance could only be bad as Alexandre and Silver Fox had definitely not reached Albany yet. To have heard from them would mean failure, and possibly, worse.

But the commandant did not have news from Alexandre. Instead, he had a favor to ask.

"I have a message that I would like to have sent to Captain Le Marchand de Lignery, the commander of all

French forces in the Ohio country. He is based at Fort Machault. Under ordinary circumstances, I would have sent Alexandre, but of course he is en route to Albany. Before he left, he told me to call on you if I ever needed a favor done that I would have asked him to do if he were here. That is why I am asking you to do this now. It would be a great help to me."

"I will do it happily, sir," Francois politely replied, "and I am flattered by the fact that Alexandre recommended me to do such tasks in his absence."

"He thinks very highly of you, lad," Captain Pouchot said kindly, "and if you carry out this task as well as he thinks you will, then I will think very highly of you too. It takes real men to do what is asked of them, and from what Alexandre has told me, you have never shirked your duty. We need men like that, son. We need them badly."

Francois started to reply, but his thoughts were interrupted by the memory of his father's voice saying, *Work hard, my son. Never give anyone a reason to call you lazy.* And then, without warning, Francois remembered something else—what his father had said after that line: *No matter what happens, always remember that we love you.* Choking back tears, Francois bowed to the commandant and left the room.

The sun was acting shy hiding behind a thick layer of clouds, when Francois and Eugene paddled away from the dock by the lower village. When he had gone back to get official directions from the commandant, Francois had asked for permission to take a companion along.

"Of course," the commandant had replied.

Francois had assumed that would be the answer, but he had wanted to check before the decision was made, for he had not yet known what the message was.

It turned out to be a simple letter to Captain Le Marchand de Lignery, confirming military support should Niagara indeed come under attack that summer. Francois's heart started thumping loudly as he heard the message, for it was then that he realized the anxiety of Captain Pouchot. The commandant was extremely worried about his post and the situation it would be in should help not arrive from the west. That was the only avenue of reinforcement, and well everyone in the fort knew it. That is why the captain sent the letter—he wanted to confirm that the other forts were prepared to dispatch their soldiers.

As Francois and Eugene paddled, they exchanged thoughts on the situation in New France. Eugene seemed to have more optimism than Francois did, and the wiser older voyageur was constantly assuring his friend that things were not as bad as he was making them sound.

"Alexandre and Silver Fox will return, Francois, and Fort Niagara is a very strong post. No, not invincible, but she will require a full military action to capture. And there is still Montreal. It cannot be easily taken either. The English still have their work cut out for them."

As Francois paddled, he thought on his friend's words. Yes, maybe there was hope for New France after all. The idea gave Francois more strength as the canoe glided upriver toward the great falls.

At the portage, Eugene and Francois landed ashore to haul their canoe up the hill. Lifting it onto their shoulders, they easily carried it up the steep slope to the top, where they laid it down to return and grab their other cargo. Once those had been retrieved, they spent the rest of the evening at Fort Little Niagara, visiting with the soldiers there. One of the Indians who was also visiting told that a great army had departed from Albany, heading for Fort Niagara. At the news, Francois's ears became alert.

"Where did you hear this?" he asked.

"The Iroquois have been discussing their allegiances lately," the Indian replied, "and I heard one of the Mohawk warriors mention it. Niagara is doomed without help."

"But if this is true, then why have we not heard about it before?"

"Because the English and the Indians are the only ones who know. The only chance of actually capturing the fort is by surprising it, and that is exactly what they plan to do."

"What makes you say that their only chance of capturing Niagara is by surprise?" Francois asked, disagreeing completely.

The Indian thought for a few moments before answering. "There are many French farther west and many more Indians. If given plenty of warning, they could easily arrive at Fort Niagara before the English. If that many warriors were to join the fort *before* the English arrived, then the forces would be the same size. Any force inside of Fort Niagara has a strong position, but it is an impenetrable one if the attacking force does not at least outnumber it. *Non*, if the English are going to take that fort, then they will have to take it by surprise."

"Until someone warns the commandant, then it will still be a surprise," Eugene noted to all assembled. "So why doesn't anybody tell him of this army?"

"The commandant has many more Indians scouting for him who are telling him the exact opposite. I do not believe that he would listen to me because I speak alone. All the others have been won over by the Mohawks. They are now agreeing to continue to give false information to retain the surprise. There is no hope for Niagara unless they can break their trust in their Seneca scouts."

Everyone around the fire nodded solemnly. For all they knew, this Indian could also be telling a lie, though most did not believe that to be the case. Still, each one had a hard time actually believing that an army was moving to attack Fort Niagara. Was that really possible? Yes, precautions had been taken, and people had lived with knowledge that it might one day come, but it was extremely hard to picture that day being so near, so real. Such things may happen at other forts, but surely not at *Niagara.* Not *here.*

In the midst of their reveries, not one of these Frenchmen thought of what the defenders of Louisburg and Duquesne had gone through and what they must have thought before their forts were taken. For no matter where a human may find himself, it is common nature for the species to think such thoughts—somewhere, maybe, but certainly not here.

20

"The falls are beautiful," Francois whispered as he and Eugene gazed at the precipice before them. They had decided to visit the cataract briefly on their way to Machault as it may well be their last chance to do so for many months. As the sun glinted off of the water, both men felt a surge in their heart, a feeling of wonder at the glorious sight before them.

"Eugene, did you believe what the Indian said last night?"

Eugene was silent for many minutes before responding to the question.

"*Oui*, I do, Francois, and that is something that I want to talk with you about. I sincerely believe that the Indian spoke truth, and I think that we should return to Fort Niagara to warn Captain Pouchot of the upcoming attack."

"But what if he does not believe us? Or the Indian? Since we were informed of the army by an Indian, would he really see our news as credible? Could we be sure that we were not wasting our time?"

"Well, I—"

"And furthermore, can we be sure that the commandant would not be upset with us for not completing the task that we were sent out to do? What would that do to our reputation?"

"I do not believe that any of this would be an issue, but I must admit that I see your point."

"And there is one more thing," Francois told his friend. "If the Indian indeed speaks the truth, and an army is coming, then it is all the more imperative that we reach Machault and secure soldiers to reinforce Fort Niagara. If we return and warn Captain Pouchot, then ultimately all he will do is send someone else to Machault to request support."

Eugene could only nod at this and agree that continuing on was their best option. Glad that discussion was out of the way, both men loaded their canoe by the edge of the great Niagara River and prepared to embark on their journey. As the boat left the shore, the woods behind them echoed a gunshot. Turning quickly, neither one could see anything, but the quick breeze by Francois's ear and the small splash a little ways off told them that one of them had been the target of the shooter. The knowledge of this made them paddle their canoe farther out into the river, out of gun range, where they stayed for some time before daring to come back to the shore. Someone obviously did not want them to secure soldiers for Fort Niagara, and the thought made them more determined than ever to reach Captain Le Marchand de Lignery safely. Niagara was under attack; they would need all of the help they could get.

When Francois and Eugene reached Fort Presque Isle, they were welcomed as friends of Alexandre's. Alexandre had many good acquaintances at this fort, and they were all glad to see his friends in their midst. Two of them offered to guide Francois and Eugene to Fort Machault, and the two voyageurs were more than grateful for their kindness.

After a three days' journey, the party of four reached Fort Le Boeuf. Located on the shore of French Creek, this fort was strategically located to guard an important water route.

"French Creek," the two guides explained, "can be paddled by canoe to the Allegheny River, and thence to the Ohio, and eventually to the Mississippi River. If this fort and Fort Machault are lost, then the connection to our forts to the south and west is also lost. It is important that we keep these forts in our hands."

Francois nodded as he gazed at the fort before him and the small village outside of it. It was beautiful to look at, and the forest backdrop only added to the panorama. If this fort were taken by the English, then Francois knew that the French would lose more than a fort, more than a waterway—they would lose one of the most beautiful regions in the country.

Francois and his companions left Fort Le Boeuf after a day's rest. Paddling two borrowed canoes for this leg of the trip, their progress was much quicker, and their arrival at Fort Machault also took three days despite the distance being longer. Along the way, they saw beautiful mountains and valleys, flowers and trees of all varieties, and many wild animals, including wolves, deer, and even a mountain lion. This last had been a real thriller, and all four men had been relieved when the lion had casually wandered in the opposite direction.

Upon their arrival at the fort, Francois and Eugene found the commandant to be away. He had left a few days earlier to visit some local Indians and was expected to return any day. With nothing else to do, Francois and Eugene made a camp in the woods and earnestly awaited the commandant's return.

While they waited, they would take small hikes through the surrounding forest. Eugene had been farther west than this point as he had canoed to Fort Detroit last autumn, but he had never gone this far west along the southern shore of Lake Erie, much less this far into the Ohio forest country. This was a first for both of them, and they each made a point to enjoy it as much as possible while they were here.

The commandant arrived about noon the next day. As he was a very busy man with many duties to attend to, he was not able to see the voyageurs until early evening, and even then, he was only available for a few minutes.

Francois and Eugene entered the commandant's office and were surprised to find the room a touch unruly. Papers and pens were strewn all over his desk, and his inkwell had many exterior stains from past spills. The lone bookshelf was piled high with stacks of books, and the small table in one corner was covered with stacks of yet more papers and pens.

The only fancy part of the room was the commandant's chair. Plush and comfortable-looking, it was the only piece of furniture—besides the desk—that looked to have come from France. Everything else appeared to have been assembled here in New France, and a sloppy job it had turned out to be.

Trying not to show their disgust of their surroundings, Francois and Eugene forced their attention to the man sitting down across the desk from them. He was shorter than most men, though not short, with a slightly bent nose. His hair was a sandy-brown color with just the slightest bit of curl at the ends, and his mustache was trimmed and groomed to perfection. His coat, though having the frills and fancy of a French commandant's, was slightly worn at the edges and faded all over. His boots were muddy, and his overall posture indicated that he was exhausted from his journey of the past few days. Overall, though, he was still a sight to see, and the voice that welcomed the two young men was one that held a real sense of authority and control.

The voyageurs were asked to be seated, but since there was only one chair in the room besides the commandant's, Eugene remained standing. Francois had offered to give his friend the chair, but Eugene had flatly refused with no other explanation given. Resigning to his seat, Francois immediately turned his mind to the task at hand.

"Monsieur, we are here on a mission from Captain Pouchot at Fort Niagara," he began but was immediately interrupted by the officer before him.

"*Oui*, and how are things going at the great fort? I do hope that Captain Pouchot and his garrison are in good health and safety?"

"Health, *oui*, but safety, *non*," Francois replied. "There are rumors of an impending attack on the fort, possibly even this summer. In fact, just a few days ago, Eugene and I heard a rumor from a Seneca Indian that there is an army already mobilized for such a task. Until proven otherwise, we feel that this rumor must be believed, or the fort may be in for a fatal surprise."

The commandant took his time in replying. The report that these buckskin-clad Frenchmen had brought him was one that came as a surprise, though it was not altogether unexpected.

"And this Indian, how do we know that he can be trusted?" the commandant asked carefully.

"Truthfully, we don't know," Eugene answered, "but what choice is there? If we prepare now for a possible attack, then we will be ready if the rumor turns out to be true. If we wait, then we will be caught totally unprepared if the same thing happens. Ultimately, I think that precaution is our best defense. The Seneca Indians are leaving us in droves to join the English, and that is a great blow to our cause, especially at Fort Niagara."

The commandant nodded, agreeing completely with Eugene's speech. However, he still was not completely sure why the voyageurs had come.

"So now, monsieur," Francois initiated, reading the officer's mind, "I would like to state our business for being here. If Fort Niagara does come under attack sometime this summer, Captain Pouchot would like to be assured of your assistance in defending it. You have supposedly promised him aid in the past, but he would like to hear it reiterated now that such an attack appears to be imminent. Here is a letter that he wrote for us to deliver, and we shall wait outside of the fort for your reply."

"I shall have a return letter ready for you by tomorrow at noon," Captain Le Marchand de Lignery told his guests, returning their bows with one of his own before they left the room.

"Well, that went better than I dared to hope," Francois told Eugene as they crossed the parade ground and exited the gate. Eugene nodded solemnly, though he too had been pleased with their short meeting. Now if only they could get a good reply to return to Captain Pouchot, their mission would have been very successful.

The reply was ready much earlier than noon. The captain called Francois and Eugene into his office and greeted them as old friends.

"It is wonderful to see you again," he told them cheerfully as they entered, "please be seated, Eugene." The twinkle in his eye was caught by both voyageurs, and they had an extremely hard time withholding their laughs.

"Well, well, how did my friends enjoy the night?" the commandant asked politely as he seated himself in his plush chair.

"It was very fine, *merci, monsieur*," Francois replied. Eugene nodded to affirm his companion's comment.

"Here is your letter for Captain Pouchot," the commandant told the men as he handed Francois a cream-colored envelope. "It explains the whole situation as I will also tell you."

Francois and Eugene waited for him to start.

"I am more than happy to send soldiers and natives to aid Fort Niagara should it come under attack, but I cannot afford to send any soldiers now. You see, I am amassing a large army at this fort in preparation of a campaign to capture Fort Pitt, the fort that the English built in place of our Fort Duquesne. I currently have about 1,500 soldiers mustered: about 1,000 French and Canadians and about 500 Indians. I plan to begin this campaign in about one month as long as I have enough soldiers and supplies ready by then. Otherwise, it will have to be later in the season, but

I do intend to again mount the flag of France over the forks of the Ohio River before winter strikes."

"That would be a major inspiration to us all," Francois stated quietly with tears forming in his eyes. "This nation is in desperate need of hope."

"*Oui*, that we are," the commandant replied, nodding his head as he gazed off at nothing. "But what am I doing? I would like to invite you two gentlemen to dine with me at noon today, and no excuses against your presence are allowed."

Francois and Eugene both assured him that there would be no excuses against their attending the meal and left the stockade, feeling very excited about the commandant's news. If a campaign could be mounted against Fort Pitt, then it would help to relieve the pressure on Fort Niagara that seemed to be mounting quickly. If it could be taken, then that would be a huge boost to the French morale. Francois and Eugene were already feeling it.

Dinner was a sumptuous affair, at least as sumptuous as a frontier meal could be. There was beef from France ("The finest in the colony," the commandant told them), duck from Lake Erie, vegetables from various gardens around the fort, as well as fresh whole wheat bread. Francois and Eugene, accustomed to corn cakes and jerky, were overwhelmed by the fare that the commandant provided for them. Making a point to enjoy the luxury, the two voyageurs ate until their stomachs were near to bursting. When they could not possibly eat any more, they thanked their host for his hospitality and prepared to leave. But the commandant was not finished.

"I am meeting with a group of warriors from the Ojibway tribe today. They are here to discuss our treaty. Three of their chiefs will be in attendance along with over fifty braves. I would like you two gentlemen to stand in my ring of officers as my honorary guests. Unless your duties absolutely cannot allow this, I will not allow you to refuse."

Of course, Francois and Eugene would not refuse such an invitation. But first, they needed to walk off some of the meal they just ate. The commandant gave his permission, and they prepared to leave.

"When do you expect this group to arrive? And how do you know that they are coming?"

"I just returned from visiting their village. I want to meet with them to discuss our situation and request warriors to help us take Fort Pitt. I do not know when they will arrive, but it should be soon."

Nodding their understanding, the two voyageurs took their leave.

21

THE WOODS TO the northwest of the fort were beautiful to behold; Francois and Eugene had not traversed this sector yet in their various explorations, and they found this portion of the forest to be their favorite.

"Look at the bushes and trees!" Francois excitedly told his companion, "they are so beautiful compared to those in France!"

"*Oui*, but aren't all trees in this new world more beautiful than those of Europe? After all, here the trees grow wild and naturally, while in France they are grown where certain rich men please to put them. There is nothing natural or coincidental about that, and I find it hard to even consider the tall plants in Europe 'trees.' To me a tree is something natural and beautiful that God placed perfectly, naturally, without any man's help. That is why this land is so wonderful, Francois. Man, nature, and God can live in easy harmony with each other."

Francois nodded at the words of his friend, for he found there to be much truth in what he had said. The trees *did* seem more beautiful when growing naturally and independently, and the trees that surrounded him now definitely fit those terms. As he looked up at the sky through the dense layer of leaves, he saw that the great blue expanse above him held not one cloud in it. Rather, the sun shone unabated on the green carpet of grass below it, making the lakes, rivers, and ponds sparkle from the rays that it sent forth. The beauty was more than Francois could even believe to be possible, and he was so caught up in the flora and fauna around him that he almost collided with the large party of Indians in the path before him.

Eugene stopped him just in time, grabbing his arm to force his halt. Startled, Francois started to say something nasty to Eugene, but Eugene's ignorance of Francois and focus on the trail ahead made Francois look where his friend did.

Then he saw them. Three chiefs decked out in full ceremonial dress that included full headdresses adorned with colorful feathers. In their hands, they carried lances, which were decorated beyond the usual weapon—these were for ceremonial purposes. Surrounding the chiefs were at least one hundred warriors, also decked out in full dress for the much-anticipated gathering. Many of the warriors carried scalps on their leather belts, trophies of past victories against their many enemies. Many Sioux and Fox heads were represented, and a few of the warriors even had blond scalps—sure signs of raids on the English settlements to the east.

As Francois and Eugene stood dumbfounded, wondering whether to talk or run, one of the warriors raised his right hand and spoke.

"Greetings, French brothers. We, the Ojibway people of the Nooke Doodem, have come to speak with our brothers the French about our involvement in the planned attack on the English. We wish to see your big chief."

"If you follow us, we will take you to him," Eugene answered proudly, turning on his right heel as he did so. Francois turned with him, and together they led the large group of painted humans to the nearby stockade where they were greeted with extreme cordiality and luxury. Tables had been set out in the parade ground, and a feast prepared for the warriors, and several blankets had been laid on the ground outside of the fort underneath a great oak tree for the chiefs to sit on. As the warriors ate, the chiefs and a few of their chosen braves met with the commandant to discuss their relationship and circumstances. Belts of wampum were exchanged, promises made, and gifts were given and received by both parties. Francois and Eugene listened with great interest and intrigue, even though this was not the first French-Indian meeting they had witnessed. It was, however, the first of such meetings that was *peaceful*. As they watched intently, they both remembered that every meeting they had seen had involved anger on the side of the Indians. Realizing this, both men began to enjoy the current meeting even more.

After the Indians had been filled beyond capacity and the chiefs had been satisfied by their discussion with the commandant, the time came for the war party to leave for their village. They had agreed to send braves to aid the French assault on Fort Pitt, which greatly encouraged the commandant. When these reinforcements arrived, his campaign forces would number close to two thousand, certainly enough soldiers to recapture the strategic Forks of the Ohio. The thought was an inspiring one as it would deal the English a blow that would greatly decrease their success of last year, and hopefully give New France new lifeblood to continue fighting.

Francois and Eugene left early the next morning, though they waited long enough to see the commandant before they left. He thanked them for their presence at his meetings: he rarely was able to entertain guests. Just before they left his office, he reassured them of his military support of Fort Niagara, should the need ever arise.

"Just give me a few weeks' warning," he joked with a twinkle in his eye. "It is impossible to move a two thousand-man army overnight!"

Laughing along with his joke, Francois and Eugene assured him that he would be informed of an attack long before it happened. The commandant nodded his assent at this, though the twinkle in his eye still remained. As he walked them to the gates of the palisade, however, his words became more serious.

"I want to thank you young men for being so sacrificial to our cause. You are both men of integrity, which is the kind of men that this land needs."

Francois and Eugene both started to protest, but the commandant was not finished.

"I have seen many men in this land. Most are looking for wealth or adventure, few are willing to work for it or give their lives to benefit this nation. You two men are completely different. You both work harder than most men twice your age, and you are both giving yourselves to help our cause. That is why I wanted you to stand by me at yesterday's council. I was proud to have you there, proud to tell the Indians that you were my companions."

"Monsieur, it was an honor to stand by *you* at the council yesterday," Francois replied, a little nervously. "Standing as one of your aides was something that I never imagined to be possible."

"It was my pleasure to give you the opportunity," the commandant replied, bowing one last time as the two voyageurs stepped beyond the walls of security out into the dangerous forest. The commandant watched from a rampart as they launched their canoes, and the two parties waved to each other before the two lone small boats rounded a bend in French Creek and were lost from sight.

22

Fort Niagara stood proudly, a large stone structure overlooking both Lake Ontario and the Niagara River. The fog hung low in the air, almost completely obstructing the view of the buildings and walls but allowing the flag to still be seen for miles. Thus Francois and Eugene saw the fort long before they reached it, as many throughout history had and would continue to do. The sight of their nation's flag still flying sent shivers up their backs. Though the chances were slim that the fort would have been taken in their absence, the visual guarantee of the fort's security reassured their hopes—the flag still flew, so the fort still stood.

"Francois! It is very good to see you!" the commandant greeted the voyageur as he entered his office.

"It is good to see you too, *monsieur*," Francois replied politely.

"I trust that your letter was delivered safely?" the commandant inquired.

"*Oui*, it was," Francois replied, "and here is a return letter from Captain Le Marchand de Lignery. He told us that an attack on Fort Pitt is being planned, but he will call it off if you need assistance. Please, monsieur, do not call it off unless absolutely necessary. Taking Fort Pitt would be a great boost to our cause, and it must be allowed to happen. Please do not call it off."

"I do not plan to call it off, Francois, but I am afraid that I will have no choice if we come under attack. Right now, we are not in danger, but once an army is mobilized, reinforcement will be necessary."

"Speaking of such things, *monsieur*," Francois remembered, "Eugene and I spoke with an Indian at Fort Little Niagara just after leaving here. He told us that an army had already started coming this way."

"One Indian told you this?" the commandant queried. "Do you have any other evidence to support this Indian's statement?"

"None at all, *monsieur*," Francois replied, "and I know that many Indians have told you otherwise, but this Indian said that many Senecas are purposely telling you false information so that the army will come upon us by surprise. We cannot allow that to happen. We must know for sure if the enemy is coming for us. And that was a couple of weeks ago that we heard this. The army will be much closer now if this rumor is indeed true."

Captain Pouchot thought long and hard about this before speaking. "So what do you propose that we do?" he finally asked quietly.

"I think that we need to send someone, a Frenchman, to Fort Chouaguen. That man will scout around, find out if an army is coming, and then return with whatever news he may have. I am sure that an army would stop at Chouaguen. There is no way they will come straight through this wilderness when a water route and friendly fort are close by. Fort Chouaguen will tell us much."

"I completely agree with you, Francois," the commandant said, "and now who should I choose to go on such a dangerous mission?"

"Well, *monsieur*, I should definitely recommend Alexandre for such a mission. He would surely—"

"Alexandre has not yet returned, and I have not heard any word from him since he left. He would not be an option."

"You could wait until he returned," Francois suggested.

"Or I could send you instead," the commandant replied confidently.

"Me? Really? I'm not sure that is a good—"

"Nonsense, lad." The commandant laughed. "You would definitely be the next-best option to Alexandre. You handled the mission to Captain de Lignery most capably, and I believe that you would handle this one with just as much skill. Please agree to go for me."

Francois was not really sure that he wanted this job. It was after all a dangerous one. But he did not feel like he was in a position to argue, so he relented and agreed to go. The commandant was delighted with his decision and thanked him many times for his bravery and sacrifice. Francois only nodded to these as he left to gather his belongings for the trip.

Early the next morning, a lone canoe launched from the dock below Fort Niagara. It was paddled by only one man as Francois had not requested Eugene's presence on this trip. He did not know why, but he had a feeling deep down that Eugene should not come along with him. Not wanting to take the chance that Eugene would be killed if he went, Francois had decided to go alone. This mission was more of a one-man task anyway. Two people would double the chances of being discovered.

As Francois paddled, he thought again of Alexandre and Silver Fox. He was getting worried about them as he did not believe the trip to require as much time as they had thus far taken. Hoping they were all right, Francois breathed another prayer for them as he paddled along the Lake Ontario shoreline.

When the sun was high in the sky and the air was as humid as a wet wool blanket, Francois beached his canoe at a place known as the Little Marsh. After eating a scanty lunch of jerky and corn and taking a long drink from one of the nearby creeks, Francois shoved off once more to resume his journey. Paddling as long as there was sunlight, he was able to paddle another six miles before nightfall. Beaching his canoe again, he bedded down for the night after a supper that greatly resembled his lunch. Tired from the long day, Francois had barely laid his head on the ground before he fell asleep.

As the next couple of days came and went, Francois found himself getting into a routine. He would rise early and launch his canoe, eating breakfast once he was on the water. At noon or shortly after, he would pause for fifteen to thirty minutes to eat some lunch and then paddle until the sun set in the evening, then he would eat some supper and fall asleep, and then wake up the next morning to do the same thing all over again. Sometimes, if necessary, he would take a small break in either the morning or afternoon, depending on his energy level.

After three or four days on his journey, Francois was almost shot by an Indian in the forest off shore. The bullet came so close to his ear that Francois felt the singe on his skin. Not wanting to take any chances, Francois had paddled farther out into the lake, well outside of musket range. Continuing to paddle eastward, he decided to wait for a while before returning close to shore. Since he was heading east, however, he did not see the thick dark clouds forming to the west. That is, he did not see them until it was too late.

A loud thunderclap behind him sent Francois frantically paddling for shore. Most people would have panicked completely and started to recklessly paddle their boat, thus sending it nowhere. Francois panicked, but he managed to keep his head focused and his paddling clean. As a result, his boat shot toward the shore with great speed, and he clung to every last hope that he would make land before the water became too choppy.

Lightning flashed behind him, then ahead of him. Two quick loud thunderclaps followed almost immediately. Then the rain began to fall. Not a heavy drenching rain, but still rain nonetheless. Francois kept his cool as he paddled toward the land, his heart thumping loudly, and his breath coming in short quick spurts.

As he neared the shore, a huge flash of lightning that made the world daylight-bright revealed a shoreline that Francois was worried he would be up against—a rocky one. As he continued to paddle, he felt a small wave rise and fall beneath him. Paddling a little harder, he managed to gain more speed. He was almost there now. If only he could...

A quick flash of lightning, a loud thunderclap, and a huge wave happened at almost exact same time, and Francois's canoe was sent catapulting over the first rocks along the shore. These ones were partly hidden by the water, but Francois could not have avoided them, even if he had seen them, because of the wave.

His boat broke into pieces, bark and log frame flying up from the impact against the rocks. Francois fared better than the boat in that he did not break apart, but he landed on one of the rocks just as hard as it had. Grabbing what belongings he could manage, he scrambled through the water to the rocks on the shore and then climbed up these to the grass.

Once he had reached the grass, Francois took off on the run for the forest about fifty yards away. When he had reached it, he slid down under a massive maple tree that had good rain coverage. His right ribs and knee ached terribly from the impact against the rock, but he did not have time to think about his pain. Grabbing a few nearby sticks, Francois worked with his flint and steel to start a fire that would enable him to see his surroundings. It took longer than usual, but after a few tries, he had a bright and cheery, if not small, fire going in the little circle he had made.

Once his fire was going strong, Francois turned to his bag of belongings. Looking through it, he found most of his items had been recovered. His bow and arrows, musket, and corn bag had all been lost; but his knife, tomahawk, jerky, flint, steel, and blanket had been saved. Thankful for what he had, Francois did something that he never would have excused himself for doing—he slept.

He awoke to the sun shining through the trees. The rain had long since stopped, though the ground and leaves were still soaked from the shower. Putting out his fire, Francois gathered what he had with him and returned to the shore where his canoe had been crushed. Wanting only his musket, he was disappointed to find nothing remaining in the small bay that he had crashed into.

Sitting down on a large rock, Francois began to think hard about his situation. He was in a bind, for sure; he needed food, and the best way to get that was by hunting. The best way to hunt was with a musket; second-best, with a bow and arrows. Knife and Tomahawk were not even worth considering.

As he thought about his choices, he also thought about which way to travel. He could continue on to Fort Oswego, practically unarmed and mostly unfed, or he could travel back to Fort Niagara. After thinking on it for a good fifteen minutes, Francois decided on the latter.

"I will return to Fort Niagara," he told himself as he stood up and prepared to start his long walk.

A new thought entered his head, and he began to think the whole thing through again.

If I return, then I will have failed my mission. Fort Niagara will not know if there is an army on its way, and Captain Pouchot will have to send someone else. Probably, Alexandre. But I am here already sent instead of Alexandre, and my position is only one or two days away from Fort Oswego. If

I return, all of my efforts will have been a waste, and I will not have helped the cause at all. I will not only have shirked my duty, but I will have shirked a duty that would have been Alexandre's. He would be very disappointed in me, as would Captain Pouchot. Is it worth it? Is it worth continuing on?

A voice inside of him told him the answer: *The New World is full of dangers, and it will not be an easy life. You will have bad times and good times. Work hard, my son. Never give anyone a reason to call you lazy.*

Francois spoke the last sentence out loud to himself as his memory voiced it in his heart.

Francois looked back one more time at the area where his canoe had wrecked and was shocked to see his musket lying in the brush on the shore! Running to grab it, all Francois could surmise in his mind was that the musket had been thrown toward shore from the force of the crash, and it had landed in the brush among the rocks and lodged there. Checking it to make sure that it was empty of water, Francois then turned to the journey at hand and was surprised to find that his mind had already been made up.

"I will continue on," he told himself as he started off to the east, "I will find out if an English army dares to move against Fort Niagara."

23

IN THE EARLY evening of the next day, Francois was startled to hear a loud snap in the woods ahead of him. Stopping abruptly, he instinctively went to the ground hoping to see whatever had made the noise before it saw him.

After waiting for close to ten minutes, Francois cautiously continued on. Watching every side of the forest for potential enemies, knowing he was deep in their territory, he was ready for an attack from any angle. The woods were extremely quiet, and Francois knew deep down that an attack was inevitable.

Suddenly, up ahead of him, Francois heard the weirdest and scariest noise that he had ever heard in his life. The closest sound that Francois could match it to was the call of an elk, but this sound was much bigger, deeper, and louder than an elk's. It also reminded Francois of a man kneeling in the bushes losing his last meal, though this sound was still much bigger, louder, and deeper.

Francois did not know whether to walk away, run away, or creep closer. He had no clue what was before him, but he was beginning to get some ideas. *Could it be the English?* his mind yelled at him as his heart thumped wildly. *If it is, then whatever would have made that noise?*

He decided to continue on. It could indeed be an English army, but Francois wanted to be sure before he reported anything to Captain Pouchot. Walking cautiously forward, he found out soon enough what he had been looking for.

A huge camp lay before him in a large meadow; tents were everywhere lined up in perfect rows by regiment. Off to one side were several larger tents that Francois assumed were those of the officers, but he had not seen enough army camps to really know about such things. At the other side of the clearing, Francois saw several cannons being unloaded from bateaux on the beach; it was then that Francois noticed the hundreds of canoes still paddling toward the already large camp.

Moving quietly, Francois was able to sneak around to the south side of this camp and found another small clearing to the east that held much livestock and provisions. As Francois stood transfixed at the creatures he was now looking at, one of them, a big-horned brute, lifted its head toward heaven and let out a loud, deep bellow. Francois jumped at the sound, but he recognized that this animal had made the sound he had heard a little while ago. Curiosity drove him to wonder what kind of animal he was watching, but he was smarter than to let his mind wander in such a direction. Bringing himself back to the task at hand, he began to analyze the camp, estimating the enemy's numbers.

While he was thus engaged, he was startled to hear a twig snap on his right. Turning swiftly but quietly, he saw the arrow fly toward him and was able to dodge it. Dropping to the ground, he loaded his musket. If the Indians planned to kill him, then they would have to fight for the privilege.

He did not have to wait long. As he loaded his musket, he saw them creep out of the woods toward where he had originally been crouching. There were four of them, and though Francois could not tell what tribe they were from, he did believe them to be Iroquois. Taking his time in loading so as to remain silent, Francois always kept an eye on their movements.

He knew that he would have to fight them. If he ran, then they would chase him, and they would surely outrun him and kill him. No, he must fight them now when he had the advantage of choosing when. As he finished loading his firearm, he hunkered down and waited for an opportunity to fire.

It came almost immediately. One of the warriors turned and looked right at him and raised its ugly cudgel as it let out a yell.

Its war cry was cut short by a bullet to the forehead. Falling down, Francois now had only three enemies to kill before taking the inevitable flight.

The other three warriors advanced quickly, hollering as they did so, and Francois met the first one with his musket butt. The warrior's nose crushed back into his skull, and he fell down to the same fate as the first one had. The second warrior came forward and wrenched the gun out of Francois's hand, but Francois's tomahawk came out too quickly for the Indian to react, and that Indian also fell with a head wound. With only one warrior left, Francois could almost feel his escape.

But this warrior did not charge. While Francois had killed these last two braves, the last warrior in the group had put an arrow on his bowstring and prepared to maim his enemy first. He had fought Mohawks with Francois before, and knew how dangerous the Frenchman was in hand-to-hand combat. As Francois tomahawked the third warrior and pushed him to the ground, this last Seneca Indian raised his bow.

Francois turned just in time to see the arrow fly. He tried to move out of its path, but the range was too close for that, and he took it right in the heart. Falling to his knees, Francois dropped his tomahawk and clutched the arrow with both of his hands. As he started to bend forward, however, Francois felt a new surge of energy rush through him, and as he pushed himself back up to a kneeling position, he drew his knife. More Indians came rushing from the English camp as the blade sliced through the air and struck the warrior's chest, opening up his heart. As the blood rushed from the warrior's body, Francois could feel his own shirt starting to moisten. Knowing that there was no chance of him making it back to Fort Niagara, Francois decided to fight until the end rather than flee. As the warriors charged, he picked up his dropped tomahawk and threw it at the first one. It hit the warrior full in the chest, and he fell to the ground just a few feet in front of Francois. Now without any weapons, Francois had to wait until the warriors came closer before he could do any more killing.

A warrior came up, and Francois shoved a stick between his legs to bring him down to the earth. His tomahawk fell right next to Francois, and he reached down to grab it. The other warriors kept coming, however, and as Francois turned back with the tomahawk in his hands, he saw another warrior standing over him, bringing his tomahawk down.

Francois felt a soft blow to the head and that was all. He did not even know he hit the ground.

Afterword

AND NOW I, the author, must explain why I chose to write a story in which the main character dies. I am fully aware that this decision may not be a popular one among readers as most prefer stories that end happily, myself included. But it is a fact that most stories do end happy so much so that sometimes even historical fiction gives up accuracy to ensure that the characters are all left alive and well.

There are many stories told of the many people who lived through tragic events and one way or another became success stories. Some found fortune, others found land or a home, some merely lived to tell of it—all survived. However, it is a well-known fact that for every person who survived, many others did not; and for every person who became rich, twenties and thirties did not. If our stories of past lives only focus on those who survived important events, then we are leaving a huge part of our nation's history untold. Every person who ever walked this land had a part in its history, and every person who lived *and* died in this land was critical in making it the countries that it is today.

This story is merely a way for me to tell how an otherwise untold story could come about, and how much a behind-the-scenes French voyageur could contribute to his nation's cause. Many such men not only freely gave up their lives but also freely gave up their chance of success so that others could live on to the next generation. And now here we are only interested in celebrating those who made it. It is well-known and often said that those who died gave up everything for us, but I think that our historical fiction does not focus on such principles enough. This story is my first effort to change that, and hopefully we will one day come to appreciate stories that retell *history* just as much as stories that retell *success*.

Glossary

Canot de Maître. Montreal Canoe, used on the Great Lakes and Ottawa River. This style of canoe was thirty-six-feet long and weighed about six hundred pounds. Cargo load was about three tons, and it was manned by six to twelve men.

Coureur de bois. "Runner of the woods." These men were independent frontiersmen who traded with the Indians for their own profit or gain instead of France's. Most of them traded for furs instead of trapped them, taking beads, blankets, knives, axes, guns, powder, bullets, etc., along with them.

Fort Chouaguen. The French name for the English Fort Oswego, which was located on the South shore of Lake Ontario on the west side of the mouth of the Oswego River. It was the central member of a group of three forts: Fort Ontario was located on the high ground on the east side of the Oswego River mouth, and Fort George was located half a mile to the southwest of Fort Oswego. These forts were taken by the French in 1756, but the commander of the French Army, General Montcalm, withdrew his troops to Quebec after the victory. The English rebuilt the Fort in 1759, and it remained until the end of the war.

Je suis désolé. French phrase for "I'm sorry."

Merci. French word for "thank you."

Metier. French word for "occupation."

Non. French word for "no."

Nooke Doodem. The bear clan of the Ojibway people. The Ojibway nation was divided into clans called *doodems*, and each clan was named after a creature. The Nooke people were the "tender" or "bear" doodem.

Oui (pronounced *we*). French word for "yes."

Sauve moi. French phrase for "save me."

Quai. French word for "dock" or "wharf."

English Translations of Voyageur Songs

C'est L'aviron (Chapter 4)

Returning from Rochelle
I encountered three pretty young ladies.
I chose the prettiest, who got on my saddle behind me.
We rode one hundred leagues without talking until
she asked for a drink.
I took her to a spring, where she refused to drink.
I took her to her father's home, where she drank glass after glass
And toasted to the health of her mother and father,
Her sisters and brothers and the one she loved.

Chorus: It's the rowing that leads us to the high country.

Youpe! Youpe! Sur La Riviere (Chapter 12)

(1st verse, in verse)
One Sunday night you see,
My friend Francoise and me
We went off for a walk to find some company.
A visit we did pay, to old bonhomme Gauthier.
I'll tell you just what happened next, but *en Francais!*

(The remaining verses, literal translation)
I lit up my pipe, speaking a few words to the people
of the house. I said to Delima
"Would you come aside, alone with me?"

"Ah, yes," she said, "with great pleasure.
You came here tonight just for fun;
You are too unfaithful to speak to me of love.
It is your little Jeremie you always love."

Let us get back to the old man, who was in bed.
He cried loudly, "Lima! Go to bed!
People of the country towns, and outskirts,
Leave because it's getting late.
It will soon be day."

I didn't wait to be told a second time.
I said to Francois, "Are you coming with me?
Good night, Delima, I'll be on my way."
I left with my hat in hand.

Chorus: Huzzah, huzzah on the river.
You can hardly hear me.
Huzzah, huzzah on the river.
You don't hear me at all.

A Saint-Malo (Chapter 16)

In Saint Malo the beautiful sea port,
Three great ships arrived.
Cargos of oats and wheat.
Three ladies were shopping.
Merchant how much is your wheat?
Three francs for the oats,
Six francs for the wheat.
That is too expensive by half.
Go up madam and see it.
Merchant you will not sell your wheat.
If I don't sell it, I'll give it away.
At that price, we can arrange something.

Chorus: We'll go on the water,
To wander around.
We'll go play on the island,
On the island.